# MASK OF DEATH

WILLIAM J. CONNELL

A Wild Ink Publishing original

wild-ink-publishing.com



Edited by Ian Tan

Book Cover by Abigail Wild

# PROLOGUE

*Meet your narrator*

***

HELLO!

It is so nice to see you. I do not get many visitors here.

Do you like stories? So do I. I have an interesting one to tell. It is called "Mask of Death." Let me set the scene.

The time is the mid-$14^{th}$ century. The black plague, or the great mortality as it is sometimes called, is in full bloom across Asia and the lands of the Eastern Steppes. I am afraid years of famine caused by poor weather and overpopulation left millions of people weak from starvation. The Black Death finds these people.

From afar, we can marvel at the great pestilence—it is truly ravenous. Once it reaches a populous spot, it spreads quickly and can render a booming trade center into an empty shell within three days.

Some say the plague is evil. I maintain it is a force of the natural world, like the change of seasons. Is winter evil? It brings the cold, and shorter days, producing soil which cannot be farmed. From this comes poverty, and from poverty comes death. Many live tortuous lives of eternal drudgery. Death from the winter, like death from the black plague, can indeed be painful, but it can also be a seen as a release from a sad life. For some, it is welcome.

Still, there is no denying that the plague inspires fear. Especially in those who have much. Life is quite dangerous as the plague does not recognize boundaries of either borders or class. Across the land, travelers journey in large numbers from the protections of one walled city state to another walled city state. They hope to escape the Black Death. But much like the ancient Arabian parable, when these travelers reach a new city, they find the Black Death is present to greet them.

In Western Europe, this plague remains a rumor, spoken of only in hushed tones.

It will not remain a rumor much longer.

# Chapter 1

*A decrepit but sprawling fortress whose name is long forgotten. Somewhere southwest of Paris, northeast of Avignon in the Kingdom of France.*

***

A PRISONER SHUFFLED INTO a darkened chamber, his arms and legs bound by silver shackles, accompanied by two guards. He was rugged and dirty with short, curly brown hair and stubble. There was a certain feral manner in his walk, in his slight hunch as he worked under the weight of the chains to put one foot before the other. But his gaze was fixed forward, never wavering.

Three cauldrons of burning fires were spread across the space, several feet from each other. Seated out of the light from the flames, on the remnants of a church altar, were eight figures, rigid and upright. The man normally had a strong vision in the dark, but this was a special place, a cursed ex-cathedral where the darkness was magically enhanced to shroud even his supernatural sight. This was the Vampire Council of the Kingdom of the Francs. Of course, they wouldn't let the likes of him see them clearly.

No matter, they had summoned him. The guards marched him to a spot centered between the caldrons, then halted.

Cesare Cattagna smiled.

"My family," he said quietly. "Is good to see you all. Especially under these circumstances." He held his hands toward the center throne and his restraints rattled. "Thank you, your sedation helped me sleep so soundly these two months. Very potent. I respect."

Out of the darkness, a high refined voice said, "Release his hands."

The guards complied and withdrew. Cesare Cattagna looked back and forth at the burning pots. "Is hot here, no? But it works."

"We've yet to succumb to the Black Death if that is what you mean to imply," the voice said. "Though we are not as strong as we used to be."

"Is regrettable, my Liege, but quite understandable."

"What does he mean to—" started another voice, somewhere to Cesare's right.

Quiet fell for a few moments before the voice in the center said, "We have not much time to idle or for meaningless outbursts. Listen well, Cesare Cattagna."

Cesare ignored the insulting use of his name, a forbidden practice among vampires except in relation to a prisoner (though, of course, that is what he was).

He shifted his feet, then stood erect.

"The truth is, the humans' misery had become our misery. France and all the surrounding kingdoms are subject to profound changes in weather. The flooding in the rivers and the rains swamp their fields, washing away crops and their precious seeds. Grains are ruined. The water drains the soil of its nutrients. Their food grows scarce, good food even more so. The number of farmable lands shrinks while their population grows, and it becomes harder to raise crops from the same soil. Less grain means their cattle and horses and chickens and all other livestock are weakened. Among the humans, the old die off along with the very young and the sick. But it takes time. There are still too many people for the land to support. These weakened people—*they* are who we feed on. So, *our* food supply is also diminished, more in quality than quantity. This impacts our people."

Cesare could already smell where this was leading. He imagined the Liege leaning forward.

"But you Cesare, perhaps you can do something. You have studied tomes and works from the best human scientists. You have made these potions and these invisible living things, what you call organisms, that both restore life or provide death. Your knowledge of herbs and plant concoctions and their effects on both the human and vampire body is unparalleled. Indeed, at least two of us on this Council owe their continued existence to you, which partly explains why you are still alive."

Cesare opened his palms. "I am your servant. But I no make the organisms. They exist. I only *enhance* them."

"You spoke in the past year of the illness they call 'The Great Mortality' or "The Black Death " on the Eastern Steppes. The disease killing so many humans there. You seem to think this can be used for our own benefit?"

Cesare smiled, revealing his fangs, thin but sharp and translucent like fishbones.

"Is a theory I have," he said. "Is easier to make something respond to something, to enhance something which exists. So, give me back a lab. Give me my equipment. Allow me my experiments. When and on who I wish without interference. I take this pestilence, this sickness to the east, and make you new, stronger version of this 'Black Death.' Its large area, the Eurasian Steppe and the Mongolian Plateau, where it has savaged for ten years, but it has still not reached here yet. It moves slow."

The magically thickened darkness could not stop his sharp ears catching a murmur amongst the Council. Good, many were recognizing his point, however grudgingly.

"The Black Death may be in Caffa. A city on the Black Sea. Appropriate name, no? I find it, I take it, and I make a new version, something much more virulent. It spread through France in two years. And, of course, I make sure it does not impact our kind, but that is easy. Our kind are fewer and stronger. We not susceptible to their diseases."

The chamber was silent after he finished.

"We know your record, maker of poisons," said a very familiar female voice from his left. "You've killed vampires, Lucien, before we finally imprisoned you. Before him, Jacme Draguignan in Marseille. Rodrigo Borgia in Milan, years ago. Many more."

"Ah," Cesare purred, "Jacme owed me and would not repay his debt. And Rodrigo—he tries to kill me first.

Who among us is not a killer when it comes to survival? Is what we are." He cocked his head dramatically as the Council hissed with displeasure and contempt. "Do I hear my lover?"

"Former," the female voice replied icily. "But my Liege, may I ask a question?"

"You may."

"Cesare, why should we give you anything when the French and English have started a war to the north in Flanders and Burgundy? Many will die. Won't it provide the same as what you promise us?"

Cesare nodded. "And who do the fighting? Their strongest. This war, they kill those who *we* most want to survive. Also—the English seem better trained and armed. They use the longbow, more powerful than the French crossbow, no?"

He made a thoughtful, clucking noise.

"I think the French lost a lot in this war. I think they fight for a hundred more years. This makes our situation even worse. But my way—the disease will kill the oldest, the weakest, and the most infirm quickly. Burgundy, Italy, Germany. The Francs. The entire Holy Roman Empire. England and the Scots. My creation will race through them in two years. Those left will be fewer, stronger. Less of them to feed will allow the survivors to grow and breed other strong members. Maybe they even stop their war." Cesare paused, letting his logic sink in. "In this case, what is good for them is also good for us."

"It is a theory, you say?" asked the Liege.

Cesare smiled again. "Yes. But a good one. When you thin the herd of the weak, you produce better food."

The chamber was silent for some time until the Liege spoke.

"You are a brilliant creature, Cesare Cattagna. You make a compelling argument. Especially impressive as French is not your native tongue. But you are not one to be trusted."

Cattagna made a mock bow. "All you say is true, your eminence."

There was another pause. Then—

"We'll give you everything you ask. And your pardon and freedom upon successful completion of this task."

Cesare smiled. "Is one more thing, your eminence."

"Of course there is. What?"

"I need to set up my lab. Far from here. At a location of MY choosing. You can send anyone with me, all you want."

He glanced toward the female voice. "Even her, if you wish. But I need to pick where to work. And I need to be far from here. I need the freedom to work where and how I deem best. In this place, I have too many enemies who might take advantage of me. When I work, I become engrossed, and that makes me—vulnerable." Cesare felt the tension among the council, cold and thick as a sheet of ice. Good. "Or I go back to my dungeon. And you can let things continue as they are."

A very long period of silence followed, Cesare waited, prepared for the decision. Finally—

"Agreed."

There seemed to be nothing more to say. As the guards retrieved Cesare and led him away, the Liege spoke.

"We will not have Carmen Teresa go with you."

Cesare smiled. "So that is what she is using as a name now?'

The female voice answered, "As far as you are concerned, yes."

He knew her real name. Now was not the time to utter it.

Cesare had gotten what he wanted.

# CHAPTER 2

*The year 1347 A.D.*

*Inside Sacra di San Michele, an Abbey in northwestern Italy.*

***

PRINCE PROSPERO MALATESTA LAY on his bed, rubbing his forehead. Lying atop him, his paramour Clarinda Corrato ran her fingers through his lush blond hair. He enjoyed the sensation of her small, soft breasts contracting against his chest while he breathed. Prince Prospero (as he preferred to be addressed) liked the way he looked. His narrow, angular face, soft hands, and somewhat slight build were unique and attractive to women. And power and wealth never hurt.

But power and wealth were no barrier to the Great Mortality that drove through the land. He sat up, and Clarinda began rubbing his shoulders.

"You seem tense today," she said. "More than usual. Why?"

"I'm worried," he said, staring outward.

The bed chamber in the tower was secluded and dark, save for a deep crenel cut into the wall. From his bed, Prince Prospero could see down into the Susa Valley and the village of Avigliana. It looked calm and peaceful. Or at least very quiet.

"Do you see any farmers out there?" Prospero asked. "Any serfs harvesting hay? Merchants leading pack mules? Pious preachers on some pilgrimage to Turin, or even Canterbury? Hell, even harlots screwing the local farm boys? Anything?"

Clarinda laughed and continued rubbing his back. "It's hard to see from here. Why don't you send some guards to beat them out of their beds? They have lazy arses. They should be grateful for your protection. Such lack of thanks. "

Prospero ran his hands through his hair.

"It's the Red Death," he said, shaking his head. "Or the Black Death, if you prefer. The people, they stay in hiding, hoping it will not reach their door. But they can't keep it out." He sighed and stamped a foot on the floor.

*(You see, dear readers, some refer to the plague as the Black Death because of the appearance of those awful black buboes on the body of a hapless victim. And some call it the Red Death because when those buboes burst, there are sprays of blood. It is also known by such names as the Great Pestilence, and the Great Mortality. Whatever its name, it is quite painful. But we shall revisit this later.)*

Clarinda laughed again, squeezing him from behind. "And you're so concerned about your people, you're such a good ruler," she said.

Prospero smiled slightly. His father, the Duke of Meriden, had been a warring individual with a fanatical devotion to King Philip. The Duke had often chided his son's lack of interest in the warrior arts. For his part, Prospero thought the earth's pleasures were limited, to be enjoyed by those who could. He thought his beliefs were validated several years earlier at Crecy when an arrow from an English longbow found a soft spot in his father's armor between the helmet and chest plate and bit deep. Thus the Duke of Meriden became the late Duke.

Prospero's own mother had died in childbirth, and his stepmother, the Lady Tremone, had died during a particularly harsh winter. His uncle, Pedro Este, ostensibly was the ruler of all these lands as regent. But the Red Death had done a great deal to diminish a man's abilities to maintain control, and the peasants in Este's kingdom were more militant than here. Este seldom ventured out, and never as far as the valley. For all intents and purposes, the area was Prince Prospero Malatesta's kingdom.

And the Black Death had been somewhat welcomed by the young prince, at first. For over a year it was something travelers spoke of in hushed voices, but it had not appeared in the Susa Valley. It kept his uncle far away. It also kept the serfs close to their hovels, too afraid to go far from their homes. For a time, Malatesta portrayed himself as an enlightened ruler, reducing the collection of taxes in exchange for the voluntary collection of foodstuffs for the common good. The village farmers rejoiced. Wars were not cheap expenditures, and the Duke of Meriden liked his fighting. The largest of the population in their donations surprised the Prince. This generosity had allowed the Prince to build a considerable stockhold of food and supplies in his Abbeys, coins in his reserves, *and* gain the goodwill of the people.

Then the plague arrived in the Susa Valley.

Many small villages were decimated. Prince Malatesta kept his stores for himself and his loyalist associates, all walled in several castle-like monasteries sprinkled throughout the province. No one would try to organize a revolt as it would require a gathering with people, and the Black Death loved gatherings of people. Now, little was still coming in. Throughout the land, all were in hiding, hoping to ride out this pestilence.

"They can't keep it out," sighed the Prince. "Neither can we. All the power in the world can't keep it away." He leaned back on the bed and put his hands over his eyes. "They say Pope Clement lives in his chambers and stays between two vast cauldrons of flames which are always kept burning. He believes it protects him."

"So do the same."

Clarinda bit his ear. "Just make sure I'm between the flames with you."

He chuckled. "How cozy, my sweet. What a quaint three we would make. You and I and Elizabeth."

A dour shadow crossed Clarinda's face. But Prospero had no qualms about disappointing her. If she wanted to be someone else's mistress, the country was filled with widowed tenants and serfs, and she knew this. She could go find another bed easily enough, and the life of endless drudgery that came with it, working in the earth until you became a part of it. But she had come too far in the past two years. She knew when Prospero had seen her working in the dirt and asked—not demanded, but *asked*—if she would like to be a chambermaid at *Sacra di San Michele*—he found her attractive. Yet she had also known she could become, not just a plaything, but a primary mistress. She knew they both thought alike, but she was quicker than him. And now, as Prospero's paramour, she lived in the rarified air of being near the royal blood without possessing any, as high a state as someone from Clarinda's status could hope to attain.

"Why not?" Clarinda said, quickly returning to her bubbly self. "I'm sure Elizabeth would welcome a threesome for a change of pace."

Prospero had indeed considered the idea, but Elizabeth was no more interested in him than he was in her. She was too strong-willed to be compelled.

Prospero took a deep breath. "Besides, imagine living in a single room, all alone but for your attendants, your physician, and your fires. It was like living in a tomb. It was better to be dead than live like that."

"So wall yourself in luxury," Clarinda said. "But do it your way."

He turned to look at her. She liked having his attention. And there was no better way to get it than to talk about his favorite subject—himself. Well, perhaps one other way, but…

"What do you mean?" he asked.

"Let's go away," she said. "You, I, and our friends. Let's leave the world outside to itself to rot and die. We'll go to our own island and bring all the food and drink and musicians and jesters we want, and we'll stay and play and make love and eat and watch comedies and let the rest of the world take care of itself until this time passes."

Clarinda watched Prospero's blue eyes light up as if a flame had been lit behind them. She couldn't control him. He had far too roving an eye for that. But on occasion, she could influence him.

He looked at her—no, through her—a look she recognized as indicating his mind's wheels were turning rapidly.

"A journey to the coast could be dangerous," he said. "It is a four-day journey at best that brings us through plague country. And which island? I own none. We would need to buy ships. We—" he paused, lost in thought again.

"Create your own island," Clarinda smiled. She gestured around with her arms. "Here. Make this Abbey your island. Invite a thousand of your most trusted knights and dames."

Prospero pondered a moment, then stood, and began to pace the room.

"We can do it," Clarinda continued. "Wasn't this Abbey built to withstand a siege? No army can climb Mount Pirchiriano. The way is too steep and narrow. We could be here a year or more."

Prospero paused at the crenel and looked outside.

"It could be a long time in the Abbey for the Red Death to pass," he said. "Months. Perhaps a year or more. We would need more provisions to survive. "

Clarinda paused a beat, then said, "We will invite others, as you said. Friends and loyalists. But no melancholy ones, only those light-hearted and hale. To gain access they will have to bring supplies. When we have those we want, we will seal this Abbey up so none can get in or out."

She smiled and tapped her finger into the Prince's back. "And we will dance and sing and laugh at the world outside until the Red Death passes."

He turned to grasp Clarinda by the arms and kiss her, biting her lip as he did so.

"Here will be our island," he proclaimed, gesturing to the stone battlements. "Remote. Castellated. And it is an Abbey, so the Lord will be on our side. It will be wonderful." He grinned at Clarinda and patted her cheek. Though her lip stung, she squealed with delight.

Then Prospero drew her close and whispered, "But of course, my dearest, we both know Elizabeth would not allow it."

Clarinda recalled the words from the oracle she consulted religiously every month. *"Opportunities are approaching—but you must proceed with caution."*

As usual, the oracle spoke in circles. But she could sense the truth. Something was coming. Clarinda saw her face reflected in a mirror and smiled.

Perhaps this was the start.

***

A lightning bolt lit up the evening sky accompanied by the clap of thunder. Elizabeth Prospero saw the storm reflected in her mirror while she combed her deep, crimson-red hair. Occasional lightning glinted off her jade ring. Once it was her mother's, or so she was told.

She liked being in front of the vanity where she could see both her reflection and the Susa Valley stretching far below. During a storm, she could sit on her marble stool and watch the weather for hours. As of late, there had been frequent and violent thunderstorms in the region, more than usual, even for this time of the year.

With the feel of a tingling sensation at the back of her throat, she reached for a linen and coughed into it. She stared at the crimson blood mixed with her spit upon the cloth, then threw it aside.

"The storm is a strong one today," said a woman's silky voice.

*Ah, Ligeia.*

Elizabeth nodded at her friend's words then slowly looked back at the mirror. The sky reflected in the glass had darkened even more. Elizabeth sat and watched more lightning flash. A pair of hands, not reflected in the mirror, gently stroked Elizabeth's neck. She felt a refreshing cold from the hands.

"How are you today?" asked Ligeia.

"I'm just fine, Ligeia," Elizabeth replied, reaching back to hold one of her hands. She cocked her head to the side, cradling against the fur-lined sleeve of Ligeia's gown. For several minutes they stayed there, Ligeia stroking Elizabeth's hair from behind, both watching the storm rage in the mirror. "But not so well as my husband and his cute little mistress."

Ligeia's hands kept stroking. "Do not trouble yourself over them."

"Clarinda and Prospero, a silly pair, wouldn't you say? They think they are hiding things from me." Elizabeth sighed, "In another time I would have each of Clarinda's arms and legs on her pert little body tied to four bulls in the village square below, and then drawn and quartered for all to see. Right in front of Prospero. It would be the appropriate message." She shrugged. "Now I don't care. I'm dying." She turned to look forlornly at Ligeia." You're the only reason I still live."

They both looked out the windows into the storm. A heavy rain had begun to fall.

After a while, Elizabeth said, "I'm scared."

Ligeia looked down at her. "I know," she said, leaning forward and kissing Elizabeth's throat. "I know."

# Chapter 3

*Blood is an omen.*

***

Prince Prospero Malatesta walked gingerly into the bed chamber he shared—at least officially—with Elizabeth. He could not remember the last night he had spent in this room, but it had been over half a year.

Elizabeth had grown cold to him. In their time apart, her once thinly disguised disdain had become more pronounced. Prospero briefly recalled how it was before. He had found her enchanting the moment they met at his father's court. Strong-willed and pretty and of a marriage-appropriate family. She, for her part, had found his occasional moments of hesitation and indecision quite attractive. Perhaps those moments had allowed her to feel more seen or heard than most of her sex, and more dignified than a field whore.

And she appreciated the roles, the lives, of royalty. Even when she agreed to marry him, she understood the Prince would have dalliances. Elizabeth had accepted this, on the condition he be discreet. Indeed, he had been in the beginning. But if he was honest with himself, he had grown less so. It was impossible to know which had come first, his carelessness or her frustration with him, but both had grown. But the inability to produce an heir—regardless of who was at fault—had driven the final stake into their relationship.

His wife sat in front of her mirror, attended by her three ladies in waiting, who all curtsied before the Lord of the Abbey. Pretty, svelte, and tall for her age Nicola, Elizabeth's favorite. The slightly shorter and ganglier Marie. And cherub-faced Rose, the shortest and stoutest.

Elizabeth's eyes flicked over him head to toe. She had a way of making him feel small without doing or saying much. "My Prince, what a rare treat it is to see you."

Prospero stood stiffly, trying to feel in control. He looked dismissively at the ladies, "Leave us alone, please."

Elizabeth seemed to try restraining a cough. Nicola, a black-haired girl of sixteen years, looked with concern at her mistress, but Elizabeth patted her elbow weakly. "Go on."

The three ladies in waiting exited the room, curtsying again as they walked past the Prince.

Prospero surveyed his wife warily, walking near the window but keeping some space between her and himself. For her part, she kept her back to him, watching his reflection in her mirror.

"Have you looked outside?" he asked. "There's no movement out there."

"Really?" said Elizabeth. "I disagree, dear husband. It rained heavily last night. The heavens opened up. The streams flow quickly."

"You know what I mean," he said irritably. "The great mortality is worsening. My stewards—those who still come back after I send them out—report our lands are more than half depopulated. They collect nearly nothing in food."

"Aren't we stocked aplenty, my lord?" There was a sarcastic tinge to Elizabeth's question. She knew well the extent of their provisions.

"Who was it who proclaimed, 'Trust me, give me your foods, and let me collect from some so there is enough for all?'" She made a mocking laugh, but a cough forced its way through, and she placed her hand to her mouth.

"You act as if you care about someone other than yourself," the Prince retorted. "You live well enough here. I don't see you in any rush to leave."

Elizabeth turned, "Why would any woman want to leave a man like you, my dear?"

Prospero ignored the slight. "I've made a decision. We are going to wall up this Abbey for a while, Elizabeth. It's safe and fortified. We'll invite our closest friends to make merry with us and entomb ourselves inside and wait for the Black Death to pass. The walls here are high and strong. The iron gates, we will weld shut. There will be no quick means of ingress or egress. Then we can laugh and sing and forget the outside world."

As Prospero walked to his wife, she started speaking, "Am I to laugh at your jest, my husband? That's ridiculous as—" but a sharp spasm rocked her, and she coughed severely into her linen.

Prospero stopped several feet away and watched in alarm. After a few moments, the spasm passed. Elizabeth tried to slip the blood-stained cloth under the sleeve of her kirtle unseen, but Prospero noticed the sanguine linen. There was also no hiding a blotch of blood on her cheek.

Finally, he said, "You should rest, Elizabeth."

Elizabeth looked into the mirror at her vanity, seeing the tell-tale blotch. She lifted her gaze to Prospero's reflection and met his fear-filled eyes.

"Thank you for your concern, my husband."

He turned his face away. He must tell Clarinda. But Elizabeth wasn't finished.

"Do you seek my approval, dear husband? I don't like your idea. Sealing one inside with no way out? That is no action of a kind and concerned ruler like yourself. And also, I fear we all might tire of our company." She paused and smirked at the Prince. "Hard as that is to believe."

Prospero waved scornfully, making his voice cold and unconcerned. "Get some sleep, Elizabeth. You look like you need some."

***

Nicola held a torch as she climbed the winding stairway known as Scalone dei Morti—the Staircase of the Dead—located in the northwest quadrant of the Abbey. Although it led to a tower providing a beautiful view of the Susa Valley below (and on some good days, the Alps), the stairwell was little used. Some thought it haunted as it was lined with niches containing the remains of monks who lived there over the centuries. Her lady was wise.

But the girl felt a chill. One moonlit night, she had ascended to the top of the tower and exited. She had seen Elizabeth leaning by a parapet beside a thin woman in a flowing white dress. The woman was pale, almost like a ghost, except for her long, deep black hair that trailed below her shoulder, a stark contrast to Elizabeth's auburn hair. She was sucking on Elizabeth's shoulder. Nicola had stepped back into the tower, but at that moment, she made eye contact with both her lady and the other one.

When Nicola met Elizabeth the next morning, the Princess had said all was well, and that it amazed her a girl of Nicola's age would possess such discretion. That was the most they had ever spoken of it.

There were two hundred and forty-three steps to be exact. Nicola counted each one until she reached one hundred and fifteen. She stopped and entered a tomb on the right. Inside, she navigated around a pair of coffins, slipped behind a tattered banner hanging on the wall, and knocked on the stone. A door slid open, and she stepped into a round, candle-lit chamber. Elizabeth sat on a small bed, holding a linen cloth to her mouth. Rose and Marie sat on the floor. To the princess's right stood

Nastagio, elderly and hunched over, wringing his hands. On her other side was Giancarlo, the bearded, black-haired captain of the Guards. Nicola thought Giancarlo had a round shape to him, but he was still a strong bulwark of a man. He wore his less formal garb, a maroon tunic belted at the waist, black hose, and boots. A short but sharp poignard was tucked into the belt.

"I was not followed," Nicola said.

Elizabeth pulled down the handkerchief, smiling.

"I know you weren't, my tall one. But as for you two—" Elizabeth gestured to Rose and Marie. "I felt it best for Giancarlo to fetch you."

"Your Majesty," Giancarlo said, nodding his head.

Nicola made her way to sit beside the princess, but Elizabeth gestured for her to sit on the ground, a few feet from her.

"We don't have much time. My brilliant husband, I suspect with Clarinda's input, has concocted a plan to respond to the Great Mortality. He proposes to invite some of his closest and strongest allies to Sacra di San Michele, have them bring provisions, and then wall us in. He wants to make this Abbey a tomb, sealed from the outside world. This is a dangerous action we cannot let happen."

She paused and waited for an objection but heard none. Rose and Marie uttered gasps while Nicola sat silent.

Giancarlo spoke first. "Life would be miserable here. And cheapened. It would be bad for everyone. In such a situation, I don't know what the Prince would do."

Nastagio raised his head. "I fear the prince's judgment. I envision a civil war erupting among us. We would be fighting for food and supplies with these guests and ourselves. And there is that dreadful plague..." he shivered. "If any of the rabble brings it in..."

Elizabeth coughed into her handkerchief. Nicola moved toward her mistress, but Elizabeth again motioned her back.

"I am sick. Hopefully not with this vile disease. But until we are sure, do not get too close to me. But yes, you are all correct. We are provisioned but an extended siege can change the people inside. And that is what it would be, a siege."

Nicola stepped back, "What do you propose, my lady?"

Elizabeth smiled. Nicola was always the most direct and practical of the ladies in waiting. Some days, she felt like the princess's own daughter.

"Giancarlo, you command our guards. Do you have enough men to rebuff people who come at Prospero's invitation?"

The captain paused, frowning and touching the grip of his poignard. "It might be difficult, my Lady. Prince Prospero is our commander."

"I don't expect you to keep all away. But find a pretense to take guards to the base of the mountain. Check others for sickness. Many can be turned away if they show signs of the plague. If you can at least slow down, or make some back, that might discourage the prince as he won't receive enough supplies which could lead him to change his course of action. He is easily distracted by trivial things. Look at Clarinda."

Giancarlo measured all of it, then stood. "We have not received any orders yet from the prince. Is this an order of yours, my lady?"

Elizabeth nodded.

"Then I shall do my best to follow them without crossing Prince Prospero."

"I know you will. You may leave. Please escort Rose and Marie back to their rooms."

The captain of the guards left with her two younger ladies in waiting.

Nastagio cleared his throat, "He is conflicted." The old man could read Giancarlo as easily as a map having watched him grow up in the Abbey since his youth.

"I know," Elizabeth said. "His loyalties will be tested. His heart may be with us, but he is in the employ of the Prince, just as his father used to captain the late Duke's guard. That is why I have made these."

She handed her physician a group of letters all marked with her seal.

"Nastagio, I am growing weaker. I would do this task myself, but my illness consumes me. All too slowly. These letters, with my seal, instruct the people to avoid contact in public places and to stay away from the Abbey. They must be distributed to Avigliana below us, and as far throughout the Susa Valley as possible. The people must be warned."

Nastagio took the letters gravely, "I will do what I can. I shall brew you some strong theriac and bring you a poultice laced with chamomile which you should press on your chest if it hurts."

"Seeing to the letters first is all I ask. But I welcome your treatment as always, thank you. Nicola, I am asking you to help Nastagio. I do not wish to put anything on you, child, but this is too important."

The oldest of the ladies-in-waiting nodded.

"Good," Elizabeth said. "This may not be enough, but it is what I have. Nastagio, please be sure to protect Nicola—and yourself—down in the village. I would like to hug both of you, but you should give me space. Good luck and take care."

# Chapter 4

*The coming storm*

***

Considerable silt and mut had accumulated at the base of Mount Pirchiriano, washed down by heavy rains. The grass was green but dotted with rocks. The pathway up the Mountain to the Abbey was littered with gravel. The sun was bright in the sky which was a rare sight in the summer of rain. Giancarlo and his men had ridden their mounts gingerly down the path.

At the moment, while his guards were rummaging through three wagons bearing the crest of the Corsi family, Giancarlo found himself facing the wrath of the clan patriarch Signore Pasquale Corsi.

"This is an outrage!" Corsi yelled. "Our family has been associated with the Malatesta family for ages. I fought with the Duke of Meriden at Crecy. I brought his body back to the family! Now you have the audacity to deny me entrance to his son's domain?"

Giancarlo kept his tone respectful but firm.

"Your apologies, my eminence. I mean no disrespect. My men found two of your daughters lying ill in the third wagon, coughing and looking quite pale."

"You have no right to bring my daughters into this!"

Corsi slapped Giancarlo across the face.

"You will let us pass."

Giancarlo rubbed his beard. Of all the disappointed, frustrated people he had turned away, this was the first one to strike him. Still, he said calmly, "You will not pass."

Corsi swung to strike Giancarlo again. This time, the captain raised his gloved hand and felt Corsi's hand hit his thick arm. The signore winced with a flinch, cradling his wrist.

"The Malatesta family appreciates all the Corsi family has done and looks forward to the days when they may be reunited with your company. But the Black Death is the ruling force now. We must act in the face of it. So, you may go wherever you wish in the Susa Valley, but my men will not allow you to pass."

There was silence for a while. Corsi started to whimper. This gave Giancarlo no pleasure, but he was resolute.

Finally, Corsi turned to his caravan and said, weakly, "I fear it is not safe for us to stay in *Sacra di San Michele*. We would be better off returning to our homes."

Within a few moments, the wagons had turned and begun traveling wearily back from where they came. Giancarlo nodded approvingly at his sentries, bracing himself. The Corsi family would not be the last party they must rebuff.

***

Nicola and Nastagio stood on a floating walkway, a string of decks lining the river, and gazed upon Lago Grande, one of two lakes in the village of Avigliana. Out there, a man in a small skiff headed across the lake.

"The waters are very still," she commented to the old physician. In two more years or less, she would be taller than him.

"Much like the town," Nastagio said. "Hardly anyone is out and about. Nor should they be."

"The fields across the lake look different."

She had seen only one worker, cutting straw with a scythe, and loading it onto a cart. "They have not been harvested," Nastagio noted. "Perhaps they started, but now the lands are untended."

The girl looked at the worker, and then back to Lago Grande. In silence, they watched the man on his skiff reach the center of the lake before he struggled with a large sack in the boat. The man finally got the first part of its contents out. Its weight dragged the rest out and Nicola gave a gasp.

Though the boat was far, she thought she had seen an arm fall out of the sack before it slipped under the water.

After a while, Nastagio quietly said, "The cemeteries are full."

Nicola looked at the physician. "Nastagio, you are old and wise. Do you believe this Black Death is caused by an imbalance in the four humors?" To her surprise, the physician laughed. She couldn't help but remember something he once said about her being a precocious girl who didn't hide her curiosity, quite like her mistress.

"I don't know. Galen said so, and he is supposed to be the father of medicine. My colleagues say to perform bloodletting. I have tried this on the Princess and it was of no use. She ordered me to stop. I have put all my efforts toward her."

"Does she have the sickness?"

"Again, I do not know. Those who do have it tend to succumb quickly. She has shown signs for months. Many more months than one should have and survived. Yet, she has sustained. I would like to think it is something I am doing, but I think not."

Nicola shuddered, recalling the pale woman she had seen sucking Elizabeth's shoulder.

"Master," came a young voice from behind them. Nicola and Nastagio turned to a servant from the Church of St. Mary's running onto the walkway.

"Father Cardone will see you now."

The three marched off the river walkway and through the mostly empty streets of Avigliana. Carcasses of pigs, hens, dogs, and goats were strewn about. Nicola put her hand over her mouth and nose. She kept her gaze ahead as she heard grunts and snorts of beasts come from some of the side streets. The animals were gnawing on human bodies left outside the doorways by family members too weak or scared to provide a proper burial.

They soon reached the Church of St. Mary's and entered through a side door that led into the Church's sacristy. The walls were adorned with frescoes depicting scenes of the life of Christ and his apostles. There they met Father Cardone, who sported a white shock of hair and beard over his red robe.

"Father, this is Nicola, Princess Malatesta's Chief Lady in Waiting."

Nicola curtsied before the priest, who said, "I am a humble priest, my dear, you do not bow to me." He thanked the young novice before dismissing him, then chided gently. "We have not seen you in church for some time,"

"I suspect it will continue," Nastagio answered. "I notice the wheat and vegetable fields are withering."

Father Cardone closed his eyes. "The Spring harvest started well. There was talk of the great pestilence, but it was a rumor, something far away. Then the rain came and flooded the soil. Many crops were lost. The people understand this, they can respond to this. Then one day in June, a farmer collapsed in the field while gathering berries. Several of his friends carried him home. They said he was vomiting blood. He died later that night. The next day, all but one of the friends who carried him the prior day also collapsed in the field. Most were dead within two days time."

The priest made the sign of the cross, clearly exhausted.

"Each day that passed, fewer workers came to the fields. By the third week in June, there were no more than three or four people still harvesting. Now, here we are in mid-July. The rain has ruined almost everything. If there is a sunny day like today, we might see one person out."

Nastagio nodded understandingly. "This is sad news, worse than I expected. But perhaps the Abbey can be of some service. Nicola, the letters please." Nicola produced Elizabeth's letters from her tunic and handed them to the priest.

"Father, we are here to ask for your cooperation with these."

Nastagio took over. "These are letters from the Princess. She commands all people to remain in their homes. The Abbey has supplies. Our plans are to try and have caravans come down to distribute food into a central place, perhaps here, and then have the people come get it. But it is essential for the people to come separately."

Father Cardone opened one of the letters and read. Upon finishing, he said, "I cannot tell people to abstain from the mass. This Great Pestilence is a scourge from God. Prayer and the Church are the only way to combat it.

You want people to stay and avoid the Church or to come here in secret, alone?"

Nastagio's voice was apologetic. "To save their lives, yes."

"Father," Nicola interjected, "this may not be from God. God wants his people to survive."

The priest's eyes warmed to Nicola. "No, my child. You do not understand. Our purpose in this life is to serve God and one another, not hide from each other. This sickness is a challenge he has sent to us."

Nastagio was about to speak but Father Cardone raised his hand. "I will distribute your letter, my friend. I and Guilliam, he who brought you here, shall post it on the doors of homes in the village and on the doors of the Church. But I assure you, most of the villagers already stay within their homes, except at night to forage for food. Of course, not long ago, our church was filled with those praying for salvation. But then the numbers began to drop. A few at first, but then many more, just like in the fields. If you can deliver food, that might bring them back. Perhaps we can work together."

"That is all we ask." Nastagio got up. "As for the food, we shall try. Nicola, it is time for us to leave. We don't want our absence noticed at the Abbey."

"Ahh, so I can assume the Prince has not committed to this scheme yet?"

Nastagio shook his head.

"Well then, you must be off. God go with you both."

Nicola and Nastagio took their leave of the priest and headed to the edge of the town where they had left their donkeys.

***

Clarinda lay on the bed in Prospero's bed-chamber, thinking back to when they first discussed the plans with the Abbey a few weeks ago. Prospero was looking out at the Susa Valley again, swirling a chalice, but he was tense.

"Who is the ruler here?" he asked.

"You are, my Prince."

Prospero whirled and threw his drink across the room.

"People are laughing at me behind my back! By all rights, my wife should be dead, but she survives and seems to be running this palace."

Clarinda reflected on this. She knew what to say – she had rehearsed it for two days. Now appeared to be a good time to speak.

"You have seen Elizabeth coughing blood. Blood has stained her cheeks. In your own words, you described her as weak-looking."

"Oh no," the Prince said turning on her. Clarinda felt her heart jump at his anger. "I never said she appeared weak. Sick, oh yes, but even still, she has a fire that burns in her. Always has. It was why I married her all those years ago."

Clarinda kept her face still. When faced with a snarling creature, one must not show fear. "There are those who are loyal to her in this castle and who worry for her. But would they be so worried if they knew how sick she was? You have said she seldom comes out of her room, and when she does it is only late in the evening. How strong would those loyalties remain if they knew she was carrying a plague?"

Prospero's glare started to lessen. *Opportunities are approaching–but you must proceed with caution*, the oracle had said.

Carefully, she added, "It is one thing to be loyal. It is another to be loyal to a person who threatens your life. You said a fire burns in her that keeps her alive. Whatever the source of this fire is, how many have it? Perhaps Elizabeth can live months with the sickness. Most of the residents of this Abbey know, deep down, that they do not possess such a flame."

***

Giancarlo paused before the double oak doors of the Prince's study, once the office of the Abbott when St. Michael's Abbey was a Benedictine monastery. He had been summoned, directed to come alone. Giancarlo was not lost on the coldness between his prince and princess. Yet he had a duty to his prince.

Giancarlo steeled himself and knocked.

"Come in," Prospero called.

Giancarlo adjusted the pommel and guard on his sword to hang at the proper angle. The Prince liked his guards to look like professional soldiers. He opened the double doors and saw, hanging over the fireplace, the shield bearing the mark of Tommaso di Savoia, the 12th century condottiere who owned and rebuilt much of Avigliana in the early 13th century. A large window on the left had the protective shutters drawn back, providing an expansive view of the Susa Valley. Immediately below, the terracotta roofs and walls of the Avigliana buildings all blended into a sea of red. On the horizon, one could see snow atop Levanna Centrale, the highest mountain among the nearby Alps.

The Prince sat at his desk reviewing some papers which he held in front of his face. He waved at Giancarlo to approach. The captain walked across the red velvet carpet in the study and stopped before the desk.

"Good evening, captain," Prospero said casually, still reading his papers.

Giancarlo nodded. "Good evening, my prince."

The Prince continued to look at his papers while the captain kept his gaze on him. A moment later, Prospero shuffled his papers.

"You've been a loyal servant, Giancarlo. Both to my father and to me. In war and in peace. My family has put our trust in you and your father before you, and that trust has always been rewarded."

The Prince stopped. Giancarlo hesitated to say anything, but the Prince did not continue. Finally, he nodded. "It has been a privilege to serve the Malatesta Family."

Prospero placed the papers on his desk, clasped his hands, and looked up. Giancarlo saw the paper on the top. He could not read it, but he could see it bore the seal of Signore Corsi.

"I understand you and your guards have been screening people to come into our little home. You have even sent some away."

Giancarlo met the Prince's eyes.

"The Princess suggested we screen all who might enter Sacri di San Michele for sickness. It is worsening in the valley, my Prince. We must be cautious."

Prospero got up from his desk and looked out to the valley.

"I know you hold the Abbey's safety close to your heart, like my father and myself. This Great Pestilence, it is a very bad sickness that kills many. Indeed, the Princess is correct in suggesting these are frightening times, that safety is under threat more than ever, and we should close our ranks and screen those who might enter the Abbey. Perhaps..."

Giancarlo grew apprehensive. The main point was about to come.

"We should screen those who are *already in* the Abbey. And if they are found sick, what do you think we should do, Giancarlo?"

The captain stood silent, desperately trying to formulate a response.

Prospero sighed and poured some wine from a flagon. "Princess Elizabeth may be sick. I have witnessed her coughing and spitting blood. Discretely, of course."

The Prince turned back to Giancarlo. "I believe you have witnessed the same, hmm?"

Giancarlo slowly shook his head, "I cannot recall with certainty, your majesty."

Prince Prospero walked around his desk and up to Giancarlo's face. "Of course, understandable, as you have been working so hard to secure our safety." He handed Giancarlo the chalice he had just filled. "Have some wine."

"To your health, my prince..."

"And to yours, my captain."

Slowly, Giancarlo took the chalice in his big hand while Prospero poured himself another drink.

After a swallow, the Prince opened a drawer of his desk. "Perhaps this might refresh your recollection." He produced a blood-stained handkerchief, embroidered with the letter "E" which he dropped in front of the captain

Giancarlo showed no emotion.

"I want to know how sick Elizabeth is," Prospero continued. "Get that old coot Nastagio and find out everything he knows. Everything. Then report back to me.

You may use your most trusted guard, but I want this done quietly. The people in this Abbey believe royal blood is free from the Black Death, and we wouldn't want to destroy that illusion."

Prospero walked behind his desk.

"I know you are fond of the Princess, Giancarlo. But if the Princess is indeed sick and it is the Black Death as I believe, I may need to take certain actions–drastic actions–to benefit the people who live here. *We* may need to take these actions. I may need you to do things involving the Princess. I want to know–is this going to be a problem for you?"

Prospero rubbed his chin and stared at the captain.

Giancarlo's mind was full of memories. He had chaperoned Elizabeth at the Court of the Duke of Milan. She was a younger, more innocent Lady-in-Waiting then, seeking his counsel on what the Prince was like, what foods and sports he fancied. In her days visiting Turin during courtship, she had sought his counsel and inquired about the welfare of the Abbey, including him and his father. One of Elizabeth's status did not usually seek the advice of a professional soldier. Or give their health more than a second thought.

The day Elizabeth stepped out of the bridal chamber in her majestic gown, she had silently held out her hand so he could escort her to the wedding. And then he thought of meeting with her and the others about Prospero's plans to seal the Abbey off from the rest of the world. That was her holding out her hand too, asking for his help, his experience, his protection.

But she was sick... his eyes had not lied... maybe with the Black Death...

Giancarlo's face did not betray any of these thoughts. "I do as my Prince commands."

The Prince seemed pleased with the response. "Then go do as I have commanded."

***

Clarinda's mind was clouded as she walked the corridor of the deepest portion of the castle, where few went. Aside from the torch she held, it was very dark. It led to an iron door that in turn opened to the outside world. She often traveled on this path. Days earlier she had ventured outside the castle walls and made a small sacrifice to the Abbey's "oracle," a blind ancient Benedictine monk who had told her the opportunity she had sought would present itself.

The monk had also cautioned she should be hesitant to take what she wanted, that her desires carried great risk. Was it Prospero's plan? The Black Death?

Someone grabbed her arm and pulled her into an alcove. She cried aloud and moved to strike at the figure with her torch, but up close it was none other than Prospero.

"Elizabeth is sick," he said in a whisper. "It must be the Black Death."

Clarinda stared at his face for a few seconds while the words hit her. There could only be one meaning of the term "sick." Elizabeth was not just ill, she was dying. It was also a question. What to do? Prospero stood nervously, twitching, his eyes darting back and forth to see if anyone was coming. As Prince, he had power over all in these lands (so long as his Uncle stayed away). Yet the walls, as they say, had ears, even down here.

Word of the plague among the royal family should not be leaked. The better breeding from royal blood created a certain immunity to the plague. At least, that is what Prospero had managed to convince the peasants of this land. If Elizabeth was sick, and if such knowledge came out, it would further erode Prospero's small hold on the people. Clarinda maintained a serious look mimicking the concern on her lover's face, but what better news could she have heard?

"What do you think you *must* do, Prince Prospero?" she asked and smiled to herself at the triumphant determination building in his face.

# Chapter 5

## *The Princess of the Abbey*

***

Sitting within the confines of a secluded alcove at the western end of the Abbey, Elizabeth coughed into the handkerchief clutched in her hand before quickly hiding it in her blouse. The herbs Nastagio had given her helped keep the spasms down for many weeks, but their effectiveness was waning. Elizabeth took in a deep breath. It felt cold in her lungs.

"Nastagio," she said gently.

Hunched over, Nastagio continued to feebly pound the herbs in his stone mortar bowl with a pestle.

"Nastagio," she said, now more a command.

Her physician stopped. He did not look up but rather stood motionless by the small altar he used as a table. His voice croaked out hoarsely. "Yes, my lady."

"Prospero knows, doesn't he?"

Nastagio shrugged his shoulders. "The prince is wise, my lady."

Elizabeth smiled at the answer, then shook her head weakly.

"My husband is not so wise," she sighed, "but he is observant, cunning." Elizabeth did not fear Prospero knowing she was sick. No, Elizabeth had never feared her husband. Quite the contrary. But knowing she was sick, and would die, and he was not, and would live–for now–that was a victory for him. And she hated handing him a victory. "How did you get those marks on your arms?" she asked, noting several new blue and purple spots on the old man's limbs.

Shame spread over his countenance.

"Do not worry, Nastagio," she said. "The Prince has suspected for some time. I forgive you for anything you told him. I know he can be persuasive. I'm grateful for the time you've helped me conceal this from him. And I know I am dying." She laughed slightly, then narrowed her eyes.

"I do want to know," she grabbed his wrist. "Why *am* I still alive? Most die from the coughing plague within hours. I've been sick for over eighty days. I have counted each day. Why don't I die?"

The physician trembled in her grasp. "The... medicine," he rasped. "It is strong. But there is... something else that sustains you."

"Something," Elizabeth sighed, closing her eyes and drifting off. "Hmm. I wonder what it is."

***

She had been toying with the jade ring on her finger while staring in the mirror for what felt like hours. Still, her restlessness wouldn't leave.

"Nicola, come closer."

Sitting by Elizabeth's side, Nicola leaned forward. Rose and Marie huddled at the foot of the bed. Nastagio stood off in the corner of the bed chamber, grinding a yellowish powder with a small stone, as he always seemed to do. A heavy rain splattered against the veranda outside her bedchamber.

Elizabeth raised her hand. "All of you must listen carefully," she said. "You may be in danger. Even you, Nastagio."

"I am too old to care," the physician said.

Elizabeth laughed. The three girls also giggled nervously, and then Rose and Marie bent forward, fearfully.

"Prince Prospero knows I am sick. He has probably suspected for some time, but now he's certain. And he knows I am weak and knows you have been with me. I fear for your safety. I want all of you to–"

Elizabeth paused. From the corridor outside there was the sound of heavy boots stepping in unison, getting louder and louder. Her ladies-in-waiting exchanged fearful looks. The door to her bedchamber opened and a slew of palace guards led by Giancarlo entered her room.

"You come into my chambers unannounced?" Elizabeth said softly, swinging her legs off the bed. She stood straight and moved between her attendants and the guards. "And all in your dress uniforms, fully armed to the hilt." She laughed coldly. "Why such formality, Giancarlo? You've never needed soldiers to visit in the past. My, this must be most important."

Giancarlo nervously stepped forward. "I have orders from the Prince, my lady," he said. "Direct orders."

"And what are they, Giancarlo?" Elizabeth stepped toward the guard. He hesitated and looked at the floor.

"I wish they were not given," he said.

Elizabeth stared at him until he finally met her gaze. Her mother had died when she was merely five, and her father always remained distant, seemingly retaining her primarily as an asset to be used to leverage a profitable exchange. For all his deficiencies, Giancarlo was the closest person Elizabeth had to a father figure.

"Then ignore them," she said. *Please*, her mind added.

The lead guard looked away.

"Prince Prospero has ordered I am to take you and your ladies-in-waiting and your physician."

Elizabeth's heart dropped but she kept her posture and expression. "Where are you taking us?" she pressed.

Giancarlo hesitated before answering. "I have been instructed to tell you we are moving the occupants of the castle to a safer location. We will escort you out of the castle."

"What is this outrage?" Nastagio bellowed, slamming his medicine down. "You do not tell Princess Elizabeth what she will do!"

The physician ran at Giancarlo, yelling. "You've been loyal to Princess Elizabeth. How dare you do this!"

"Back down, old man," Giancarlo's second said, but Nastagio pressed on.

"No, you bastard!" Nastagio yelled, slapping his weak hands at the guard captain. "You may assault me, but this is the Princess of the Abbey."

Giancarlo seemed frozen in shame, but his sergeant shoved Nastagio to the ground.

"Be quiet old man," The man said moving towards Elizabeth, who crouched to help her physician up.

"Be quiet?" Nastagio stammered as he rolled on the ground. He struggled to his feet and spoke louder. "Be quiet? You come here in the darkness of night to hide your deeds. Be quiet? I will not be quiet."

"This is your last warning," the sergeant said, making eye contact with one of the guards carrying a glaive, a tall polearm with a sharp blade on the end.

Nastagio continued, "Help us! The Princess—"

Giancarlo finally seemed to wake up. "Just restrain—"

The guard lowered his glaive and thrust it into Nastagio's back. The blade burst from Nastagio's sternum. Some of the blood splattered onto Elizabeth's clothing. Nastagio vomited a few moments before his head dropped to his chin. The guard lowered his weapon, and

Nastagio's quivering body slipped off the blade and onto the floor.

Rose and Marie screamed, but Elizabeth raised her hands and gestured for them to be silent. She was stunned. Nicola simply stared at the guards. The room was silent except for the sound of Rose and Marie whimpering.

Giancarlo dealt the man a backhand across the face. "Did I give that order?" He glared at his sergeant who seemed to shrink at his stormy face. After a minute, Giancarlo said to Rose and Marie, "Get a new dress for Her Majesty."

Elizabeth raised her hands, and everyone stopped. "That won't be necessary," she said as she knelt and placed a hand on Nastagio's neck. "Goodbye, old friend." She turned and went to Giancarlo. "So that is how it is to be, Giancarlo?"

Giancarlo gestured to another guard. "Bring the body."

***

The guards hustled the girls and her majesty out of the bedchamber and into the catacombs of the Abbey. Rose and Marie were crying softly in the back. With Nicola trailing her, Elizabeth walked along between two guards.

She was familiar with every inch of the castellated Abbey, much more than Prospero or any of the servants. They were going down a shaft dug into the mountain, an area left untouched for the most part except for furtive ingress and egress. Clarinda haunted this passage, as Elizabeth knew from having observed her several times in secret.

A pang of regret went through her. *I should have strangled Clarinda when I had the chance.*

The corridor opened into a chamber dimly lit by candles. At the far end, an iron door stood open. Outside the exterior world was cool, even though it was mid-August. There was a fog out, but in the background, one could make out a few trees that had survived. A light rain fell and there were a few outer garments laid out on the floor of the chamber.

"May I assist the girls in dressing?" Elizabeth asked.

"Yes," Giancarlo answered.

Elizabeth fitted a long, hooded, purple cloak onto a tall, thin Nicola, then leaned back and said, "This is beautiful on you." She wrapped a blue coat around Rose and tightened the cinch at the waist. "This will keep you well." Lastly, she draped a brown heavy surcoat over Marie. "This is the perfect color for your eyes."

Giancarlo held up a black, fleece-lined overcoat, and Elizabeth allowed him to put it on her.

"Thank you, Giancarlo," Elizabeth said, pulling her hair so the long, red tresses hung over the collar. The captain gave a half smile. Elizabeth added, "I know you are conflicted over this, but remember, from this day out—" She reached forward, and touched Giancarlo's cheek before saying, "Today you chose a side." The guard's face turned crestfallen, and he stepped back.

Several servants stood by the doorway holding massy hammers.

Elizabeth said, "I see. Send out the last of the sick and seal the exit, is that it?" She laughed bitterly and turned around to see her husband in the shadows. Though it was dark outside, Elizabeth could see very well in the dim candlelight of the chamber.

"Giancarlo, will you please usher my ladies-in-waiting outside?"

Giancarlo nodded, and he and two other guards began to move the girls to the door to the outside. Marie and Rose sobbed more hysterically, but Elizabeth said, "I shall be with you girls, just give me a moment." Nicola grasped Elizabeth's hand, but Elizabeth mouthed to her "Go on," and the guards walked her out. After the three girls were outside, Elizabeth said, “My dear husband, I am so happy you interrupted your busy schedule to see me off.”

Prospero’s face was unreadable. “I’m sorry, Elizabeth.”

“So am I,” Elizabeth said. Her thoughts turned to when they first met, when the prince was indecisive, and how that seemed both amusing and appealing. Prospero had grown.

Elizabeth felt a series of coughs coming on. They were violent, forcing her to bend at the waist and draw her hands to her chest, but the spasms passed. Then she stood erect and adjusted her jade ring so it sat properly on her finger. Even after all the indignity, she was still of noble birth.

Elizabeth saw Clarinda trying to hide in the dark behind Prospero.

“She’s dead,” Clarinda whispered into Prospero’s ear, but Elizabeth heard her quite distinctly.

“You are right, Clarinda,” Elizabeth said. “I am dead. But do not be afraid. You are the Princess of this Abbey. You’ve presided over it and you’ve certainly bested me. You’ve taken my place. I honor thy royal blood with a kiss.”

Elizabeth kissed the fingertips of her right hand and blew it in Clarinda’s direction.

"As the Princess of the Abbey, this is yours. Rule well, my sweet."

Then she walked outside.

***

CLANG!

The heavy iron gate shut behind them. Nicola looked at her mistress. Rose and Marie wailed loudly, slapping their hands against the door.

Rain had been falling but now there was a fog surrounding the women and the animals that had been left for them–Elizabeth's brown gelding and three donkeys for the others. Some servants had left some bundles on these and two wine flasks. Food and water, how kind.

"Let us in!" Marie sobbed. From the other side of the gate came a loud battering sound.

"Do not strain your voices, they cannot hear you," Elizabeth said. "They are hammering the door shut with iron bolts. This way is sealed."

She wrapped her arms around Nicola who stood with her head bowed, staring at the earth. Elizabeth gently tightened the strings on the cape over the girl's shoulders. Pangs of regret went through her as she looked at the girls. They had been loyal to her for several years. Perhaps she could have sent them to another location earlier and avoided this. Prospero had proven to be more decisive on this point than she anticipated (with no small help from Clarinda). But no matter. What had happened had happened. Now they were alone in a plague-infested world.

"It's time to go," Elizabeth said finally. Nicola shuddered. Elizabeth felt a cough coming but stifled it. "Marie, Rose, we must leave."

She walked over to Marie and Rose and touched each on the shoulder. Rose was on her knees, crying into her hands.

Marie was curled on the ground by the door. "I've done nothing!" she screamed. "I'm not sick! I'm not sick!"

Elizabeth whispered to Rose that it would be all right, then helped her onto her donkey. She had to try several times before Marie got up and also mounted her donkey. Nicola was already on hers. Then Elizabeth mounted her horse. The four rode off, Rose weeping, Marie still moaning she was not sick, Nicola and Elizabeth in silence.

She took one final look at Sacre di San Michele. One could tell it had once been an Abbey and had been hardened into something more like a castle. Fortified towers with arrow slits strategically cut into them. Spiral staircases within those fortified towers. Parapets topped with battlements. The uniquely curved walls, originally built to have the Abbey fit atop the mountain, now providing an almost unassailable front for any attacker. Yet it had also been her home for years. The place where she was courted and married. The place where they held Christmas Eve feasts for the villagers of Avigliana. Where she made plans for her future and for the futures of her ladies-in-waiting. She had especially watched Nicola grow from an infant into an inquisitive and astute, yet discrete, eligible maiden. Saint Michael's Abbey was... unique.

And this was the last time she would ever see it.

*Death, even when you come for me–which no doubt will be soon–I shall not forget Prospero with that simpering Clarinda behind him. If revenge from the grave is possible, I shall have it.*

A thunderbolt crossed the sky above them and the light mist turned into heavy rain.

# Chapter 6

Giancarlo and his second were outside the walls of *Sacra Di San Michele*, behind the towers. It was a small stretch of ground, not far from where they had pushed out Elizabeth and the others a few hours earlier. Gloves covered their hands and masks covered their lower faces. Nastagio's body was draped over the back of a donkey. A stream flowed from the castle down the mountainside, and this area was strewn with rocks. A few small trees grew there. Not many liked the altitude and the buffeting winds.

The second, a man named Santi, cursed when his blade struck rock.

"Damn, why are we doing this? Nastagio is dead."

"Because you acted without orders and killed him," Giancarlo retorted sharply. "He was a skilled physician. A loss to the Prince and the Abbey. So, now you do as I say."

Santi tried to work his shovel around the rock. "The ground is too muddy and rocky," he grumbled

With considerable effort, Giancarlo managed to remove a shovelful of mud and stone. He paused after the exertion.

Santi studied Giancarlo's face. "The Prince wanted Nastagio disposed of. Alive or dead, he did not care. This is no time to be sentimental, my captain. Or for misplaced loyalties."

Giancarlo took in the import of Santi's words. He was right. And so was Prospero. There was no doubt Princess Elizabeth Malatesta had been sick. Both the ladies-in-waiting and Nastagio had spent time with the Princess, much more than Giancarlo. What had been done had to be, regardless of personal thoughts.

"The longer we stay with this body, the greater OUR chances of getting sick," Santi spat, throwing down his shovel.

Giancarlo dropped his shovel and stepped in front of Santi, looking down on him. "Do you want to challenge my authority, Santi? No one else is here." Giancarlo touched the pommel of his dagger. "Now is your chance."

Their eyes met.

"No, captain, I do not challenge your authority. But the Princess is gone. There is no question about who rules the Abbey. And I believe Prince Prospero demands unwavering loyalty. He wants this body disposed of outside the Abbey. He doesn't care how. I think for us, the less time with this body, the better."

Giancarlo held his ground. "The reason we are out here is because you didn't follow my commands. Nastagio had served Prince Prospero, and his father before him, as well as the Princess. The man was skilled and wise. He had a great medical mind. And he was a man of peace. Men like him are not easily found. For him to die like that at the end of a glaive..."

He shook his head, his heart heavy with sorrow and disgust. "If we get sick from his corpse, it is your fault. You can dig and finish the job."

Santi held Giancarlo's gaze for a few moments. Giancarlo's muscles tensed, ready to draw his weapon. Then the second shrugged, "As you command, Captain."

Santi leaned down and resumed digging. After watching for a moment, Giancarlo joined him. They managed to reach some solid dirt, dug a shallow grave, and moved Nastagio's body into it. As they shifted rock and mud onto the grave, Giancarlo's mind traveled.

Nastagio had been a good doctor because he was not afraid to challenge the traditionally accepted beliefs.

He believed the way to treat a person first involved taking the history of a person's health, followed by a thorough investigation of the body. He critiqued the commonly used practice of bloodletting to address illness, preferring to experiment with herbs and other substances. Nastatagio was ahead of his time. A kind and faithful servant to the Abbey. His administrations had saved his father's men after a few harrowing brigand skirmishes, and even his father. The physician had so kindly given him, barely a grown man then, no small number of reassurances about the wounded. Those like Santi were too young, too new to remember. He ought to have told them more of these stories...

As for him, Giancarlo... Nastagio's and Elizabeth's faces floated back to him.

*You've been loyal to Princess Elizabeth. How dare you do this!*

*Remember, from this day out, today you chose a side.*

What would his father think of this innocent blood on his hands? Giancarlo shoveled dirt, rock, and mud onto the doctor's body.

"*I've condemned them all to death,*" he thought. "*Call me Judas.*"

***

Elizabeth led the girls to Avigliana, at the foot of the mountain, all the while carefully rationing their food and water. The last time she was there was the spring before she showed signs of sickness. Then Avigliana was a poor but still inhabited village with some sense of honor and ritual in place. According to Nastagio's last visit, Father Cardone presided there when Nicola and Nastagio visited about a month ago. Elizabeth's heart sank at the memory of a halberd bursting through her old friend, but they had no time for sentimentality.

Perhaps Father Cardone could be of some help.

She found the inhabitants dead either in the streets or their beds. If there was a living soul, they were well hidden save for rats scurrying through the streets. The beautiful Piazzas, Sana Maria, and Conto Rosso were filled with turned-over carts and wagons, corpses between them. When they went to the Church of Saint Mary's, they found the pews filled with the dead. Flies and other insects seemed everywhere. The cold body of Father Cardone lay collapsed on an altar while his novice was in the adjoining room. After much searching, they found a cottage with two empty beds, and there they made their place for the night. Elizabeth in one bed with Rose and Marie in the other as Nicola lay on the floor wrapped in a fur rug. Elizabeth told her she could stay in her bed, but the lady-in-waiting would not do so.

Unbidden, an old tune her mother had sung to her many years ago came floating back in as she lay on the bed, fidgeting with her ring.

*My daughter, I pray ye say,*
*As thou art to me dear,*
*How shall I serve ye to thy pay*
*And make the right good cheer?*

Nothing more came back to her.

As she lay, Elizabeth stared at the jade ring for some time and tried to remember–unsuccessfully–the remaining words of her mother's song.

During the night, Rose and Marie suffered several bites from fleas jumping onto them from the woolen blanket they lay under. A few also found their way to Nicola.

Elizabeth was left untouched. As she drifted off to sleep, she thought of Ligeia. Would she appear to her again?

***

They could have stayed in Avigliana, but there was no food to be found, only rotting corpses or the very sick, which terrified Marie and Rose. Not that they saw many. The handful of people in the village were ensconced in their hideaways. On the third day, Elizabeth left with the girls. As they passed by Lake Grande, they saw bodies had been collected along the shoreline.

Days stretched on as they moved aimlessly, desperately through the valley in search of shelter and food. Everywhere they went there was more rain, more death. Twice they came across coffins in the woods. Apparently, wolves had broken into them and bodies lay around the half-eaten corpses pulled from the boxes. Rats must have come to feed on these, but somehow, they died too. Occasionally, they found a chicken or a rabbit roaming on its own, which they captured and ate as best as they could. But by and large, they saw few living creatures. And while Elizabeth had learned to hunt as a royal, she was weak. Prospero had been right; the land had been ravished by the plague.

Slowly, they grew disoriented.

Rose was the first to be stricken. One morning, when the rain had paused and they prepared to set out from a peasant house, Rose complained of chills. By midday, the group stopped because of her crying. When they pulled her off her donkey, they noticed a purplish splotch on her neck. Nicola and Marie recoiled in horror, but Elizabeth sat by her, stroking her hair and repeating that all would be well. Still, Rose was unable to be comforted and cried throughout the afternoon and evening until she breathed her last breath sometime near midnight. When Elizabeth inspected her body, she found purple blotches all along the inside of her thighs and under her arms. They used tree branches to make a shallow grave for her. Nicola lay a small bouquet of posies atop the pile.

The next two days brought more wandering in damp weather until Marie slipped off her donkey in the early evening. When Elizabeth and Nicola came over to her, they found her dead, her skin as yellow as dandelions, eyes staring heavenward. There was a stench of sweat and excrement about her. They had been so lost in their wanderings they had not noticed. Elizabeth directed Nicola to walk away while she dug another shallow grave. Then she accorded Marie's body as much dignity as possible, closing her eyes, tying up her dress, and brushing her hair. Alone, she dragged the body into the grave and then had Nicola come over to pay her final respects before they covered it with mud.

By morning, all of the donkeys were dead as well.

Two more days passed with on-and-off rain. They tried to find natural canopies from the trees. Elizabeth and Nicola rode together on her horse, coughing and sneezing. They slept on the floor of the woods, falling asleep because of exhaustion. They may have been in these lands before, but alone, in the rain, with a constant fog, and weak with hunger, they were disoriented and could get no bearings. But they pressed on. There had to be someplace they could go.

Mid-morning one day, overcast with a hazy sun, Elizabeth walked in front of the horse while Nicola sat on it alone. Nicola coughed up blood which splattered onto Elizabeth's shoulder.

Elizabeth paused and felt a chill. It was the *sound*. This was the coughing plague, the most lethal form of the Black Death. The kind which racked Elizabeth's body. While force she did not comprehend kept Elizabeth alive, Nicola did not have that protection.

"I'm going to die, my lady," Nicola cried. "I don't want to leave you."

"There is a village just a little way from here. We'll get you there and you can rest. There is an old woman, one who is good with herbs. Hang on." Or was this old woman still there? Still alive? Or maybe she left long ago... Elizabeth's mind was hazy.

Leaning off the horse, Nicola said, "I cannot."

"You must," Elizabeth said. "I order you not to die."

Nicola shook her head. "I once asked... Nastagio... how this Black Death began..." Her voice sounded dreamy.

"I won't accept your death," Elizabeth said, but Nicola had slumped forward on the horse's mane. "But he did not know..." the girl slurred.

Elizabeth tightened the string of Nicola's coif. She grabbed some brush and tied Nicola around the waist to the horse. Then she mounted the animal, sitting behind Nicola's body, and began to have the horse trot. In the thick mud, progress was slow, but after an hour they had covered more ground than they could have while walking. Elizabeth was confused. The area was vaguely familiar. Where was that village? She went to the place she thought it would be but–nothing.

Then their horse died underneath them.

It did not stumble or give any warning. It collapsed mid-step and fell on its side. Elizabeth, sitting farther back on the animal, was able to roll off before the creature fell, but Nicola's right leg was caught under the horse's body. Nicola made no sound, unconscious. Elizabeth struggled to pull Nicola out from under the animal and lay her on a soaked bed of leaves. Blood trickled out both sides of Nicola's mouth, and her right leg was bent. Elizabeth checked the leg–it was injured but not broken.

Elizabeth looked around for shelter when Nicola suddenly vomited an explosive torrent of blood, spraying Elizabeth. For a moment their eyes met.

Elizabeth watched Nicola's pupils grow smaller, the life behind them departing.

Elizabeth pulled Nicola close and began to cry. The blood on them both was no matter. This end was inevitable.

"It's all right," Elizabeth said gently. "It's all right."

After a while, she lowered Nicola to the ground, closed her eyelids, and looked for a few stones to cover the body.

***

Time passed. The Prince had only sent a few messengers to close allies they wanted. As Prospero and Clarinda expected, that was all that was needed. Word traveled far and quickly of these plans and many wanted to wait out the great pestilence in the Abbey. Small groups and larger caravans arrived, much more than the limit of one thousand people the Prince had set with Clarinda's guidance. Each person passed his watchful eye and the even more discerning eye of Clarinda, the woman referred to in hushed whispers in darkened corners as the new Princess of the Abbey (though none dared say it loudly).

A few maids and kitchen staff somberly missed the principled, pragmatic Elizabeth and knew she would not stand for the insensitive decadence while the commoners huddled sick and starving in their homes. Giancarlo watched bitterly too. Nastagio's words nagged at him.

*I fear the prince's judgment. I envision a civil war erupting among us. We would be fighting for food and supplies with these guests and ourselves. And there is that dreadful plague... If any of the rabble brings it in...*

But there was nothing left to do. If he died... well, he deserved nothing less.

Close friends tried to offer great amounts of portable wealth, but Prince Prospero had little interest in these and turned them away. Fortunately, he had a sufficient personal guard to address any problems. Food and wine were desired. Animals such as pigs to be consumed were prized, and well as those such as goats and chickens who could provide replenishable nourishment. Persons skilled in trades, such as carpenters, builders, and blacksmiths, especially those with their own tools, were also sought. A few barber surgeons gained admittance. Finally, artisans. There was no certainty as to how long they would be entombed in the Abbey. The Prince wanted his days filled with entertainment.

Oh, the occasional comely face that caught the Prince's eye might also be allowed entrance, of course, but Clarinda managed to keep those to a minimum as the Prince's reliance on her grew. Within three weeks, *Sacra di San Michele* welcomed over a thousand of the heartiest, and most well-provisioned, of Prince Prospero's friends.

# CHAPTER 7

*An abandoned, fortified manor house with an exquisite exterior now in disrepair, located in southwestern France, west of the Durance River.*

***

CESARE BORGIA WAS WORKING furtively over a table. He didn't have much time. The Council was on the hunt. The vampire wore leather gloves that went past his elbows, a cotton facial mask, and an oversized white woolen surcoat splattered with blood stains. He poured a lime green potion into a vial and then reached for another bottle containing a brown elixir, which he also emptied into the vial.

"Good," the vampire murmured as the contents of the vial turned a dark purple. "Maybe this time you work."

The Vampire Council wanted its antidote, all right. This is why he escaped to the secret laboratory, enchanted and protected by hostile spirits who surround it. His current project went beyond what he had discussed with the Council two years ago. Both vampires and the Church would pay dearly for it.

Cradling the bottle carefully, he carried it to another table where there were several large, glass lenses. Borgia cautiously poured the purple liquid into a glass bowl which held a black substance, then placed it under a finely ground lens magnifying the image of its contents.

He clasped his hands watching the purple and black liquids swirl around each other.

*Go on, fight. Fight to the death.*

The liquid concoction turned into a brighter shade of purple. The mixture held its color for a moment and Borgia smiled.

But only for a moment.

The color darkened, black rising from within. After a minute it all turned pitch black. Borgia stared for several moments, then laughed.

"You consume all the others. I made you too strong, my pet."

He recalled taking samples of blood from dead Mongol soldiers encamped outside Caffa. He realized then, the Great Pestilence was lethal and growing more so. If anything, he had underestimated its capacity to mutate. It was not difficult to enhance since it was already strengthening itself. Cesare merely accelerated the process, dispersing the result into a nearby tributary that fed into the larger Durance River, the dominant riverway in the region.

For good measure, he spread the result into the wells of the nearby town, especially near the Jewish synagogue, a place where he had found a tunnel allowing him to slip in and out unseen at night. Travelers frequently passed through, resting before making their way west to Europe or further east on a pilgrimage to the Holy Land. Taking his creation with them.

Only he had done too good a job.

Borgia remembered his initial time watching a respected village elder return to life, after having just expired from the plague. He had watched the man's life drain out, his head slumping over. Then, with surprising speed, the corpse became reanimated, its limbs twitching while Borgia stared in fear and fascination. A moment later the... creature raised its head and launched itself at him.

Only his vampire reflexes and the thing's ungainliness saved him. Somehow he outmaneuvered the former elder, trapped it, and managed to cart it back to his lab where he studied it for many days until it finally crumpled again.

Over time, with other specimens, the vampire scientist learned that the new virus strain was so powerful that it was causing this phenomenon. The dead were brought back to life, lacking nearly all their previous faculties but the instinct to consume. These "fleshers" could rise either quickly or over a period as long as a week. But they needed to feed. Their metabolism burned, and without food, they perished. Plants didn't interest them. They enjoyed vampire flesh as much as human to the mishap of a couple of his former guards.

What a fortunate accident for him. The antidote to the original plague would pale in value after this started spreading. His value to the Council would only increase. Against their will, of course.

He walked out of the room into a larger chamber. Row upon row of large cuboids of reinforced glass, each approximately seven feet high, three feet wide. It was a long and costly project years ago, but worth it now.

Each block contained a human in varying degrees of decomposition. Men. Women. Children. Borgia gazed over the bodies and shook his head. His efforts at developing an antidote to this latest situation had not been as successful as developing the enhanced version of the plague. But soon... soon.

He went into another still larger chamber. The room had one small chandelier at the top and only a pair of flambeaus burning in the corners, harder to see in. There were some of the same cubes there, but a brown tint over the glass obscured their contents. His most current experiments.

Borgia peered close to one. Something inside crashed against the glass but it held. A woman pressed against the surface, biting the cube wall with her fangs.

This did nothing but produce bleeding from the gums.

Borgia studied her like the lab experiment she was. "I know it is not as pleasant as being a guard at the Vampire Council. But then again, you volunteered to watch over me. I am sure they thank you. And take comfort in this. If we find a cure for this Black Death–you will have been a part of it."

Borgia walked away, various combinations and calculations running through his head.

# CHAPTER 8

*Into the countryside*

***

FOR AN UNKNOWN LENGTH of time, there had been heavy rains. The kind of rains with a sky so dark it was hard to tell day from night.

Elizabeth staggered through the woods. Ligeia had abandoned her. She had not eaten for two days. Her friends were all dead. Soon she would join them.

The sound of the rain pounding fiercely on her head was maddening. Though she pulled up her hood, the woolen coat was becoming soaked, and the weight of the rain being absorbed in the cloak was pulling against her. She wasn't thinking, she was stumbling, falling, rambling through the countryside. Finally, she crumpled on a rock beneath a towering oak whose branches provided some shelter.

She lay her head upon the cool stone. "Take me," were her last thoughts before she drifted off.

***

Elizabeth awoke startled. She felt certain that when she last laid down it would be her final rest. Yet her body would not die. Why? Why did the coughing sickness take so many so quickly, but she was allowed to linger?

She was also hungry.

It was close to dusk, and a thunderstorm rolled in. Sharp lightning bolts gave some illumination, and she saw she had stumbled into a clearing filled with graves of some nameless village. Graves? Dumping ground was more appropriate. At one time efforts had been made to bury the dead, as indicated by primitive stick crosses stuck in the field. Farther along there were small tell-tale mounds of dirt, shallower graves, that much had been washed away. Body parts protruded from these mounds. Small limbs often ended in stumps that had been nibbled on. Animals too were starving, and meat was meat.

Elizabeth traveled along the edge of the field until she saw the body pit. As the plague took greater control in a village, the term "burial" lost its meaning, and the only thought of the survivors was to be rid of the bodies. This led to the dead being carried and tossed into large pits, which grew larger each day. Before Elizabeth, a sea of corpses writhed in a large trench, moving and rocking. A few wooden crosses mark the edge of the pit. Water must be pooling underneath, moving the bodies.

Then a spot caught her attention. Some of the bodies were not sliding along carried by water but instead were–pulsating.

She stepped closer.

There was another flash of lightning.

Something was alive, or at least not dead yet. It was a man, or what had been a man, clothed only in braies from the waist down, hunched over on all fours, rummaging through the pile. The man pulled his head out of the chest of another, chewing on a body organ. There were gaping dark holes all over him where buboes had burst.

Elizabeth screamed but caught herself. She held her breath, forgetting her hunger and exhaustion. Maybe the man had not heard her.

Its head went into the air like a dog sniffing the wind.

Then it turned in her direction.

Elizabeth remained frozen in her place.

The creature had seen her. It began to move in on all fours in her direction, not quite running yet but still moving at her.

Elizabeth knew she was dying. And she did not want to die this way. But she was too weakened to move. If now was the time for Ligeia to save her...

The creature continued its progress towards her on all fours, unable or unwilling to stand, but it moved nonetheless.

They made eye contact.

Suddenly, Elizabeth saw–herself. She was looking at her own visage through the eyes of the creature. What sort of hallucination was this?

The man had stopped just at the wooden crosses on the outside of the body pit. He had sat back on his buttocks in a crouch, staring emptily at her.

The rain continued to beat on them both.

Just as suddenly, she was back in her own mind again. The man-thing came out of his stupor and began to scramble toward her.

"Stop!" Elizabeth threw out her hands.

The man halted, only a few feet from her.

For a second time, she saw herself as if she had jumped back into the creature. This time she was aware, in some sense, she was in its mind. She couldn't read it, no, but she felt sensations and urges. The overwhelming feeling was of hunger, and of an instinct driving to pursue her. She also felt decay, pain–of blood throbbing through torn veins, of flesh breathing, and of a pulsating brain.

Unsure of what was happening, she focused on the beating organ, tightening her fist.

*Leave me.*

The creature staggered backward. The pulsating in the brain stopped. It collapsed and hit a rock, splitting its skull open. Brain matter oozed. The eyes closed, and the mouth gaped open. Within moments, the rain had started to fill it.

Elizabeth coughed again. And again. The creature lay motionless on the ground. Whatever had just happened, she was still dying. And where could she go? Where could she go to die?

She closed her eyes and whispered, "Ligeia–where are you?"

***

What drew her, she did not know. She floundered through the woods, her body torn by branches and thatch, stumbling, falling, crawling, for hours. Her mind was unfocused, and she only followed some sense that pulled her along. Somewhere she lost her coat, it had slid off her thin body. The rain had continued to beat on her and bodily fluids ran from every orifice. Somehow, she found herself against a great wall covered with brush. She pulled the growth aside and saw there had been something engraved on a door, but it had been chipped off and was no longer eligible.

With all her remaining strength, she pushed it open and entered.

A coldness permeated the air of the mausoleum. Elizabeth felt it pass as she walked down the cement stairwell. At the base of the stairs was a mirror, its frame lined with fanciful cherubs. She was compelled to look.

Staring back at her was a sickly hag with long, tangled hair knotted with mud and filth, her cheeks hollow and sunken, deep circles under her eyes.

She went into a corner and sat with her arms wrapped around her knees, shivering in the dampness. The cut marble of the crypt floor was cold. Her clothes were soaked completely from the rain and her own perspiration. Three candles burned over an ancient mantle.

In the center of the room, a finely adorned coffin made of mahogany sat atop a slab of marble. Amidst coughing spasms, her mother's old tune floated back. This time, she began singing.

*My daughter, I pray ye say,*
*As thou art to me dear,*
*How shall I serve ye to thy pay*
*And make the right good cheer?*
*All thy will*
*I would fulfill–*

Elizabeth's body rocked with the song. This time more of the tune and verses were coming back. Her eyes were kept trained on the mahogany coffin laid out on the floor across from her, the lid beginning to slide.

*Thou knows it well in ffay–*
*Both rokke ye still,*
*and dance the year till,*
*and sing 'by, by, lulley, lulley.'*

The pain in Elizabeth's stomach was overbearing. She lay on her side but continued to sing.

*Mary, Mother, I pray ye,*
*Take me up on loft,*

*and in thyne arm*
*Thow keep me warm,*
*and dance me now full oft;*
*and iff I weep*
*and will not sleep,*
*Then syng 'by, by, lulley, lulley, bye bye.'*

The lid slid more. A slender, bony hand reached and pushed the lid farther back. It moved smoothly along its grooves. A figure wearing a white burial shroud arose from the coffin.

Elizabeth stopped singing. Instead, a shrill hum came from her throat.

The figure dropped its shroud to reveal the ivory body of Lady Ligeia. Her white tunic only heightened the ghostly aura, broken only by her sharp blue eyes, sanguine red lips, and dark hair.

Ligeia stepped from her slumber chamber. Elizabeth kept humming and rocking, but she clasped her sides tightly.

"You came," said Lady Ligeia. "Of course. I should have known you would."

Lady Ligeia floated across the room. Elizabeth was shivering, wracked by a series of convulsions. She began to retch.

Ligeia gazed at her for some time. Then she reached and touched Elizabeth's taut, gnarled belly. Elizabeth's teeth chattered. Ligeia said nothing but continued to inspect her body, touching various spots with delicate efficiency. Elizabeth was aware she was being touched but could not feel the contact.

"My late husband was a physician," Ligeia said. "Didn't I tell you that?"

"I-should-bbb-dead," Elizabeth spat through chattering teeth. "As are Marie. And Nicola. And Rose." Her eyes met Ligeia's and the question did not need to be spoken.

"Because of what I have done," Ligeia said. "What I did was wrong, for you," she paused, stroking Elizabeth's hair. "And for me."

Elizabeth convulsed again, imploring with her eyes.

"I knew you were sick," Ligeia said. "Even before you knew, I saw. The laws of my kind say I should have let you die, that I should not have intervened with one dying from plague. But I couldn't let you. I'm sorry."

Elizabeth shook more violently now, and her body shifted on the floor. The entire cold seemed to penetrate her.

"So now, I've poured some of my kin into you. My blood has kept the demons in your blood at bay. At least till now. But the Red Death is powerful."

"Help me," Elizabeth whispered.

Lady Ligeia stroked her hair some more. "I cannot bring myself to kill you. And I cannot fully heal you. I can only give you what I can."

The two stared at each other for some time before Elizabeth silently nodded.

# Chapter 9

*Rebirth*

***

Heat. A fire that seemed to consume her.

Ice. Cold so intense she could not feel her limbs.

Elizabeth tossed and turned in a feverish sweat. Her body lay on a cot set in a small alcove at the side of the crypt. Heat and cold racked her body in bursts, some lasting seconds, some minutes. The changes were abrupt, extreme, and her body shuddered with each one. At times she would drift into unconsciousness at times. Colors exploded over her. Great round shapes of intense colors filled with black streaks. They seemed like living entities exploding from within.

And they were.

Buboes arose from her skin and then erupted, spraying fluids and pus. She could see it, but the pain was so numbing she felt none at all. However, the realization it was her body gave her nausea and revulsion. A constant swirling sound filled her ears, and it was all she could hear until it blended into the background so she no longer heard it. Images of Ligeia over her, beside her, with her, yet nowhere. Pain too intense to experience, pain that had become consuming.

The cycle repeated itself.

Again.

And again.

The colors changed, the images moved, but the shift between heat and cold was constant. Buboes would erupt underneath her skin, explode, and her old skin would slide off, revealing a pristine new layer only for that layer to have buboes reappear. Ligeia was sometimes in a white gown, sometimes dressed in black, sometimes covered in blood. One last time Elizabeth had an image of Ligeia's face above her–it appeared to fade into the image of a skull. Then blackness.

Elizabeth felt no pain. Silence surrounded her. She looked down upon–a nude figure, covered with scratches, bleeding profusely. Elizabeth's own face, reposing, her arms crossed over her bosom, at peace. Elizabeth felt herself withdrawing upward, further away from the scene as both figures diminished in view. The nude figure looked up. Elizabeth could see–it was Lady Ligeia, her blood-filled mouth agape, displaying her fangs. A high-pitched shriek tore through the crypt, though its origin was not evident. Ligeia threw her upper body onto Elizabeth, and as Ligeia did so, Elizabeth's view furiously descended down to her own face. She was going to crash into herself. Just before she went into her face, her eyes sprang open.

Then nothingness.

# CHAPTER 10

*Growing pains*

***

AT FIRST, SHE STAYED in the mausoleum. Wrapped in a woolen blanket, on a small bed, tucked away in an alcove off the main chamber, she lay exhausted on her left side for... days? Weeks? Unable to eat or move. No solid excrement (though an occasional urine release). Periods of lying awake and periods of sleep. It was some time before she became aware she was clothed in a white cotton undertunic. And it seemed her tunic was always fresh like it had been changed while she slept.

She did nothing, except listen. Her hearing was sensitive. What little daylight filtering through from the crypt's door above bothered her. The cool of the night was more relaxing than the heat of the sun, even though it was in the transition of fall.

At times she heard scraping and footfalls behind her, possibly of Ligeia coming and going. She guessed it was at either dusk or dawn.

Once, without thought, when Elizabeth heard the sounds, she murmured, "Hungry!"

There was no response other than a pause in the footfalls.

She drifted back to sleep. Then, something stirred. Again, she heard something behind her, not footsteps, but as if something dropped. With great effort, she rolled over.

A dead possum lay prostrate on the floor about ten feet away.

At any other time in her life, it would have been cause for disgust, but she did not feel that now. Elizabeth crawled out of the bedding and onto the cold floor. She dragged herself over to it. As she drew closer, she could see it was panting. She heard its heart beating.

It was not so dead. And this made her crawl faster.

Upon reaching the not quite dead animal she bit deep into its belly. Blood spurted all over her, but she did not care. She gouged on the creature's entrails. The more she ate, the more she wanted to eat. She had no thought but to consume, picking through the bones for the inner organs, cracking open the skull to reach the brain.

Later she dragged herself back to her bed, her hunger only somewhat sated. As she lay there she briefly wondered how she could bite and slice so quickly through the creature's skin. She glanced down and saw her white shift was covered in blood. Her hands too, the once lustrous jade peeking through a coating of dull brown. Then she slept.

At some point she woke, wearing a clean nightshirt.

***

More time passed.

She slept most of the time but stirred at dusk. Occasionally, a wild animal would be left for her, in a nearly (but not quite) dead state. Small animals. Squirrels, possums, rabbits, some large rats, maybe a cat. Every time, she would feed. At first, it was the same. She would crawl over and then eat with fanatical abandon only to return in a crawl back to her cot. One time there was a fox, warm and large. Without thinking, she found she was able to go over on her hands and knees. When she ate, it was deliberate.

Sometimes, she used her fingers to feel along her teeth, her jaws, and the muscles surrounding them, all of which seemed to have strengthened. She did not have fangs, but her teeth seemed stronger, she could bite through skin and bone.

A time passed and her appetite grew as the small game satisfied her less and less. There was no repulsion at how she ate–everything left for her was food.

She also found herself growing more restless. At night she got off the cot and paced the floor of the crypt. Ligeia was never there. Elizabeth wanted to go out and find her but was hesitant to do so. One night she resolved to stay up until Ligeia returned, but as dawn approached, she was overwhelmed with an instinct to sleep. She would curl up on her cot and hope to find food later. However, when her clothing became saturated in blood, she would wake up wearing a clean undertunic or shirt. She noticed a green ring on her finger. What was it? For some reason, she did not take it off.

More wild animals were left on the mausoleum floor near her which she would find and eat. But the animals had grown smaller and smaller. One day a robin. One day another squirrel. These were eaten quickly and did not sate her hunger, but merely sustained her.

Then one day, the food stopped appearing.

***

Her first instinct was to stay in bed. This she did for a period. Most of the day and into the next night. It was not so much she saw light, but she had a sense of night and day. She could hear different animals and tell which were nocturnal and which loved the sun. There was a pace, a rhythm with the way blood flowed through day versus the creatures of the night.

Daytime unsettled Elizabeth while night felt more comfortable to her. On one such night, hunger got the best of her. She walked up the crypt steps and returned to the outside. Small woodland creatures were in the area. Elizabeth could make out the distinct aroma given by a pair of chipmunks nearby and underground. She could tell when they were about to pop out of their burrows. She could hear the heartbeat of a thrush sitting in a berry bush, thumping furtively, hoping she would pass. She could see the end of a squirrel's tail behind a tree.

The first few times she reached for the animals they evaded her, and she returned instinctively to the crypt before dawn, ahead of the disturbing sunlight. There was no food waiting. She lay on her cot, hungry, and frustrated.

The following night she became aware of wind in the air drifting toward her and this wind carried the scent of everything, including herself. The smaller animals knew this and were acutely attuned as a predator approached. Elizabeth practiced maneuvering with the airflow. And hunting barefoot allowed her to move more quietly. While many creatures escaped, her skills as a hunter increased each night. Animals could be distracted, like humans, and not be as alert as they could be.

She devoured her prey quickly, her jaws able to tear through muscle and bone with ease. Hides and skin were not satisfying, and neither were bones. Even though she could grind them with her jaw, so she avoided eating them. Only muscle and organs were food and these were sustenance of the most minimal kind.

One time while hunting, she found a stream in the area. Her eyesight was so much better than before, with just a sliver of the moon out she could see pike, trout, and perch floating in the water. At night, these fish, if not asleep, were docile. After a short while she learned of the deeper pools where the fish liked to congregate. She became adept at kneeling by these places, reaching in and snatching the fish from the water. Fish were easy to eat, and she especially loved consuming the front of the fish where its brains were lodged. This food was superior to rodents, but still just enough to keep her going. Her hunger never became sated.

There were many things Elizabeth had forgotten. Her past was murky, though she always knew how to return to the mausoleum. On occasion, she would raise and notice the green ring, images of her walking in some dark corridors, much like her tomb but even longer, flashed in her mind. But these would quickly dissipate.

Lady Ligeia was never there, or if she was they never met. But one evening when Elizabeth awoke, a set of clothes was laid out for her including a black, fleece-lined overcoat that seemed familiar, though she could not place where from, as well as clean undergarments and close-fitting hose and tunic. This night, as before, she ventured out. Something inside her felt different.

***

It was cooler now, the fall season, perhaps winter, and some of the trees were losing their leaves. She preferred the cool time. Elizabeth was thinking how pleasant it felt to have the clay squeezed between her toes. The branches of the fir trees rustled under a strong breeze. Elizabeth turned in the direction of the wind and stretched out her arms, letting the damp air cleanse her skin. It was such a wonderful sensation.

She walked through a small meadow of poppies. Flowers which had closed for the evening lined the path, though some moon lilies bloomed vigorously. She was acutely aware of their color, and to a lesser degree, their scent. The moon lilies were fine. But the posies were sweet, and not in a pleasant way. No, it was slightly sickening. Still, it was mild enough.

Moving through the woods, she sensed something new in the area. Something larger than the usual forest creatures she'd been finding. It gave off a whiff of sweet perspiration. Elizabeth moved quickly and stepped into a clearing.

It was a small encampment by a stream. Two young muscular men, one bearded the other not, sat on logs directly across from one another, a fire burning between them. A large fish, a pike, was set on a spit, cooking over the fire. A third person was sleeping on the ground, a woman by the looks of it, mostly covered by a blanket. The men wore nondescript cloaks suitable for the cool fall air, and the bearded man wore a straw hat.

Elizabeth stood at the edge of their small clearing, her arms at her sides, her head cocked to her right side, twisting in jerkish movements to see each person. The two men stared back at her, startled, but not quite fearful.

"What have we here?" the clean-shaven man asked. It was in Italian, but not a dialect Elizabeth recognized. She barely made out the words.

This speech caused the sleeping woman to stir. She looked at her two companions, then saw Elizabeth. The woman suddenly reached for a hand axe and started to rise, but the clean-shaven man touched her arm.

"Take it easy," the clean-shaven man said.

Elizabeth stared at them blankly.

The woman crouched on the ground, gripping her axe tightly, "She's evil! Can't you see–she's evil!"

The bearded man rose to his feet, looking down at Elizabeth. He was at least six feet tall. "I think she's just a lost soul," he said. Elizabeth's head jerked upward to look at him. "My sister is easily startled," the man said. He extended his hand to Elizabeth."We have some nets set up by the river. We're just hunters in waiting."

Elizabeth took the man's hand and held it. Again, she noticed her green ring as the flames from the campfire danced off the stone.

"So am I," she said. It was the first time she had spoken in a long time.

Then she bit the man's index finger off.

***

It was all so clear. The bearded man staring in shock at his hand with the finger missing. The other man, seemingly slow to move, bending for the axe his sister held. The sister preparing to scream. Elizabeth knowing what they were going to do before they did. The clean-shaven man rising from the log with the axe, his jugular throbbing his heart pumping and blood flowing. Elizabeth leaping forward and driving her teeth deep into those delicious, bulging veins.

The sensation was true satisfaction.

The man dropping the axe, then falling onto the fire, breaking the spit. The sister, on her feet, taking the axe and swinging. Elizabeth turning the brother's body so that the axe strikes the back of his skull and becomes lodged therein. Grey matter seeped out.

Elizabeth wiped her hand on the man's back and put her hand to her mouth. Brains. Delicious!

The girl screamed, turning to run. Elizabeth watches her go away, then jerks her head to the bearded man, his eyes open incredibly wide. She can hear his blood pumping too. Part of her wanted to pursue him, but she smelled the dead brother's brains and could not resist. She kneeled down and reached into the skull and pulled out more gray matter to eat. Scanning the ground, picking up a sharp rock that surrounded the fire, bashing the dead man's skull, and picking the loose bone apart so she could devour the entire inside. It was nourishing.

Watching the bearded man out the corner of her eye back away while she enjoyed a feast. He ran from the scene.

After eating her fill, she returned to her mausoleum and fell asleep feeling satisfied.

***

Elizabeth awoke the next night with a mild hunger. She thought of yesterday's kill. Kill? No, it was merely feeding. Eating had been satisfying.

She walked toward the stairs of the crypt, brushing against the cherub-lined mirror at the foot of the stairs as she did so. Outside was a cloudy night. Cool again.

Pleasant. Her first thoughts were, *Where had she gone last night?*

Sniffing the air, she could recognize scents that refreshed her memory. Food was out here. She walked toward the stream and reached the camp from the previous night to find the body of what had been the clean-shaven man. The arms and head were separated from the torso. Either she had eaten more than she remembered, or the animals had taken what she did not. Probably both. There was not enough left to eat. Even if there was, these remains gave a noxious odor to her. The living flesh of a fresh kill–that's what she wanted.

Something drew her to go further down the stream. In the distance, she could hear animals moving, hunting, dying, but all seemed to scramble away from her path. Even though it was cloudy tonight, her eyesight was keen in the dark. The pale glow of a cloud-covered moon gave her all she needed. After a while, the stream turned to the right, but she continued along.

Ahead, she found her destination.

A small round clearing emerged from the woods, at the base of a hill. She came at this time because–she wasn't entirely sure. But some instinct drew her here.

In the center of the clearing was a rectangle of loose earth piled to form a small mound. Within the rectangle, a form was rising and then sinking beneath the earth. This happened again. And again. Elizabeth stood by silently.

An explosion of dirt. A hand bursting through the earth. It reached open-palmed for the air, motionless for a few seconds. Then there was a thrashing of loose dirt and rocks as what lay underneath climbed out.

A younger man clad in a hose and an overtunic gingerly climbed up and crouched on the mound, his head swinging back and forth in a vacant, rocking motion. There were no burial shrouds here. He, like so many others, had been tossed into the graves en masse, with no preparation. His body was covered with large and oval purple and black blotches where buboes had exploded from within.

Elizabeth took several steps towards the man. She reached out to it. Not physically. Mentally. How she did not know, but she did.

The creature's mind, or what was left of it, was a jumbled mass of synapses and tissues, much of it maggot-filled. It was not aware of what it was. There was no memory, no thought–it was like the slate that Elizabeth's teachers had used to educate her in–where?

Who? It is only a faint memory, a shadow from long ago. Yet Elizabeth sensed, somehow, that like those tablets, the slate–what it *had* been could be written on. By her.

"Come with me," she said.

The man stiffened and began awkwardly shuffling, following her out of the clearing.

# CHAPTER 11

*Followers*

***

SHE WANDERED THE COUNTRYSIDE, resting in caves or under fallen trees during the day, and traveling at night. These travels lasted several nights, as she went farther and farther from the mausoleum and Ligeia. More and more she found mass graves. Often there were piles of bodies in towns where people had grown too weary to bother with burial. Sometimes there was nothing. But other times, there would be a stirring. On occasion, she found a wanderer. She could not raise the dead, but when she found them, she could see into their minds. How, was unclear. But she learned how to direct them.

The undead did not respond to complicated commands. Sometimes she could get a sense of a memory, something that had been imprinted on the brain long ago. Sometimes the creatures she found were so gone that she could do nothing with them. Still, Elizabeth began to develop a small group that stayed with her.

Once, with a group of a half-dozen flesh eaters more or less in tow, a slim, undead woman came running out of the dark and right at Elizabeth. Elizabeth knew–she KNEW–this woman intended to kill her. She was... familiar. It was the sister, the one who had slipped away the night Elizabeth had first fed on her brother. The "hunters in waiting," as they called themselves.

*Die*, Elizabeth thought, but the woman kept coming, impervious to her directions. When the woman was upon her and grabbed Elizabeth by the throat, she suddenly found herself in the woman's head.

Elizabeth commanded her to stop.

The creature abruptly halted but continued to look at Elizabeth hungrily. Elizabeth's eyes grew burnt orange. The sister released her grip and dropped her arms limply to her sides. Elizabeth reached further into the woman's mind, directing the woman toward a great oak tree. Elizabeth moved her body back, and the woman creature drew her head back as if in pantomime. Then Elizabeth thrust forward, and the woman did the same, impaling her skull on a tree branch protruding from the oak. The limbs of the body quivered for a while and Elizabeth studied it closely until it grew slack.

Elizabeth waited to allow the ones following her to see the body hanging flaccidly from the tree. There was no capacity for reasoning within them. But even the undead had a desire to feed, a form of self-preservation. Elizabeth had the power over the most primal of urges, the urge to survive, and while the flesh eaters did not understand her, they did respond to her. That was enough. For the moment.

Elizabeth ate fruits and nuts and vermin she found. Until one day she discovered she had much sharper senses and could smell plants and insects, besides the small woodland creatures all around her. None of it was filling for her or the growing band of followers.

But it kept them going.

***

She learned. When hunting or fighting, the way to stop her followers was to destroy their brains. Physically shatter it.

A stab to the heart. A bear bite on the thigh. An arrow through the gut—none of those things "killed" them. Oh, they could expire, from hunger. Their bodies were always warm, burning inside, and their hunger was a driving force. A good feeding could let them go on for several days, some more than others, but eventually all would grow weak if not fed again. Elizabeth had a different stamina, but she too felt weak after not feeding for several days (she was more skilled at capturing small animals than the others).

One thing puzzled her. Her people might have a very basic sense instinct of se-preservation, but they would jump heedlessly into certain destruction when feeding. It was like the blood from a fight overcame the instinct, and they could not see a danger to themselves. Except for Elizabeth.

She realized this after the boar attack.

On one evening, her group, now over twenty members, found a wild boar with an injured leg. They formed a circle in her direction and descended on the boar like a pack of wolves. But wolves will attack a formidable prey with smarts and strategy, and instinctively one will draw its attention, while another attacks its weak side. Elizabeth's creatures ran upon the boar all at once. It speared some with its tusks, snapping their bodies, but the others kept biting and groping the animal. They paid no heed when one of them had their head caught and ripped off from the boar's tusks. The boar's jaws bit off a creature's hand, and the creature kept coming with the other. All that mattered was the insatiable drive to consume. When the creatures smelled blood, even Elizabeth could not pull them off. Eventually, after losing a few more members, the horde dragged the boar down and devoured it.

They tore into the flesh of the beast even as it quivered in death spasms. It seemed for some, the power that re-animated them also strengthened their jaw muscles. As she ate, Elizabeth did not think it odd, but only how the food was unsatisfying to her cravings.

However, the band did fear Elizabeth. On some level, though their minds were gone, they saw what she could do. She had the power to make the creatures destroy themselves, to violate the one powerful and surviving instinct of self-preservation.

They would rest during the day. Elizabeth forced them to. Left to their own, the creatures would wander aimlessly, perhaps finding a meal, perhaps finding nothing. Some still did leave. If a creature got too far from Elizabeth, she lost her control over it. In that case, either they found food or they kept wandering until they dropped. Prior to the Black Death, there would have been many pilgrims in the area. But the lands had been depopulated by the great mortality, though some folk still made their treks through the dangerous lands.

***

Prospero. Who was he? A vague memory.

Elizabeth was uncertain of many things, but she did know she hated the name. Especially when she glanced at her ring. She did not particularly seek or ignore the ring, but when she focused on it, it brought images of walking in the catacombs of some faraway place, and "Prospero" was a part of it.

Then one night while walking ahead of her group, she came across another woman, a girl on the cusp of womanhood. She was a flesher, like Elizabeth. The girl was hunched over and hobbling about on one foot, dragging the other behind wrapped only in a tattered purple cape with a hood over her head. Something was familiar about the girl. As Elizabeth approached her and drew the hood back, the person struggled to lift her head. The face of a sixteen-year-old girl looked up at Elizabeth, her countenance covered with abrasions, and one eye blind, but Elizabeth recognized her.

She brushed the girl's hair back tenderly. "Nicola."

Nicola stared at her blankly with one good eye. Elizabeth probed her mind and found her to be just like the others.

Somehow, Elizabeth felt sadness. She brushed Nicola's hair again and walked past her.

Elizabeth stopped and looked at the crescent moon. A pain spasmed throughout her body like the impact of an arrow. So much came back to her jarringly. Her husband. His mistress, Clarinda. Giancarlo. Nastagio. Marie. Rose. And poor Nicola. Elizabeth stroked her chin and laughed to herself as her mind came alive with memories and emotions.

*What am I?*

There were footfalls behind her. Her people must be moving along.

Elizabeth turned. Nicola was right there, head bowed, reaching out to touch Elizabeth's arm.

"Nicola?" Elizabeth probed her mind again. There was no mind to speak, but there was... something. An... attachment... to Elizabeth.

*Loyalty?*

It was then Elizabeth learned even when the mind did not survive death, select emotions–strong, genuine, deeply held feelings–might survive, in some bare form.

Elizabeth broke a small tree branch off and made a strong wooden splint, binding it to Nicola's injured leg with vines. The leg was no better or worse than when Elizabeth had buried her.

*Well, it had been a shallow grave*, she remembered.

Now, Elizabeth did not feel quite as alone as she had been. And while her thoughts of the past were usually shadows, seeing Nicola brought back what had happened to her, what had been done, and to Nicola and Rose and Marie at *Sacra di San Michele*. And her words about returning. She recalled how she felt as the vaulted door was hammered shut behind them that night.

She remembered her words about returning.

*I have unfinished business there, and I must attend to it.*

# CHAPTER 12

*Dreams of color*

***

PROSPERO STIRRED IN HIS bed. Something had awoken him. He sat up and looked around. It was the former bedchamber he had shared with Elizabeth.

He glanced at Clarinda beside him, her features barely visible in the candlelight. She was emitting noises through her nose he had not noticed before. They bothered him.

From behind the door, outside of the bedchamber, he heard several voices calling his name. Haunting voices. Yet vaguely familiar.

"Prospero," said one.

"Prince Prospero," said another.

"Prince Prospero Malatesta," said a third.

Unable to resist the voices, Prince Prospero got out of bed and walked—no, *glided* across the floor—and was at the door.

He opened it.

Blinding white light filled his eyes, and he threw his arm up to shield them.

*Where is this coming from?*

The light faded. This was not the corridor, but a room bathed in a dark blue light. On the floor was a thick blue carpet.

"Who is there?" he asked cautiously. Was he dreaming still?

"It is us," said several voices.

He turned.

Three women sat next to each other far into the room, their heads down. Each was dressed in royal gowns made of blue. They looked familiar but he was not certain. He stepped toward them.

"Who are you?" he asked.

"Ones who you know," said one who sat on the far right.

She looked up.

*Nicola!* His late wife's lady-in-waiting, the one she seemed to favor.

"Ones who you have known," said the second, raising her head. *Rose!*

"Ones who walked here before," said the third, following suit. *Marie!*

Prince Prospero shuddered and tried to move back from his late wife's ladies-in-waiting, but he found himself transported forward.

"Have no fear," said Nicola.

"We are not who you think," said Rose.

"We are here to help you gain what you desire," said Marie.

The girls stood up together and walked single file away from him to the opposite side of the blue room. Prospero followed, but he did not feel his feet moving. No, he was... floating. Before his eyes, the girls disappeared into the blue. He threw his hands up as he reached the end of the room. He was going to crash into the wall.

Yet, he did not crash. Instead, he turned on his right side into another room. Purple. Like the other, it had a deep and thick carpet, the light coming from the braziers burning behind stained glass. The girls were farther ahead of him, their gowns now colored purple, still walking in a line away from him. Prospero called out, but the figures disappeared to the left. Again, he glided forward, faster this time, and turned abruptly to the left. He was in a bright green room. This time the girls were even farther ahead than before, dressed in green, before they disappeared. Once more he was propelled forward and, just as it seemed he was going into the wall, he shifted to the right into a room bathed in orange. Of course, the carpet and the clothing on the girls matched.

"*It is one great hall of many chambers,*" he thought. "*Each lit with the flames behind stained glass. Each apartment in the hall breaks off at a sharp angle so I cannot see where the next room is until at the end.*"

The colors of the rooms were intoxicating. Upon entering the next succession of rooms he only caught glimpses of the ladies in waiting as they disappeared into the next section. Orange turned into a white room, and the white into a violet room, a shadowy combination of blue and purple. The violet room turned into–

His body jarringly halted.

At the end of the violet room, Prospero had come to a solid black wall. Gingerly he reached to touch it–and his hand did not stop.

Prospero lurched back. It was not a black wall, but a completely black room. And it felt cold.

"Why does Prospero not enter?"

It was the voices of all three girls, speaking at once.

Prince Prospero rubbed his hands. "This last room," he said, "it is all darkness."

The girls spoke again in unison. "There can be no light without darkness."

"And what is in there?" Prospero asked.

The girls repeated, "There can be no light without darkness."

Prospero turned to the three who sat on the rug of the violet room.

"Why do you show me this?" he asked.

"Is Prospero not bored?" asked Nicola.

"Does Prospero not tire of monotony?" asked Rose.

"Is this not what Prospero wants?" asked Marie.

Prospero ran his fingers through his hair. Now capable of moving on his own, he retreated back through the violet room and into the white. In each compartment the flames grew as he entered, the colors dancing on the walls. The movements fascinated him. He continued to retreat back the way he'd come and the rooms and colors collided in his eyes. He could still hear the voices.

"Prospero shall desire this," said Nicola.

"Prospero shall build this," said Rose.

"Prospero shall have this," said Marie.

The voices pounded in his head, the colors swirling around him in a blur, and he felt himself falling. He was in his bed again, sitting up. He felt his nightshirt wet with perspiration.

Clarinda opened her eyes. They met his own with concern. "What is it?"

Prospero laughed. "A dream," he said. "A wonderful one at that."

He reached over to hold her chin. Clarinda felt his grasp uncomfortably strong, but she did not change her expression.

*Her face was much prettier before*, Prospero thought. Then he said, "I've grown bored." He leaned into her chin. "But I was just given an idea to add some color to this place."

Clarinda hesitated to speak. Prospero wasn't releasing his grip. "By whom?"

He grinned. "From some late friends of ours."

# Chapter 13

*Old friends, new friends*

***

One night followed another, but now the quest to feed was accompanied by a conscious effort to seek out more of her kind. Elizabeth controlled a group of near fifty. She wanted more. Typically, they would wander until they found a village. The plague had taken many, but they found places with a few isolated individuals to feed on. Her group continued to hunt awkwardly, not as a cohesive group. When Elizabeth was strong she could concentrate enough to command the group to surround a small hamlet and close in on it, but the further her people were from her the harder they were to control Those in close proximity were the easiest. Her results were inconsistent, but she was getting better.

Since Elizabeth's people traveled best at night, the living they did find were often trapped in houses. These people were almost always immediately descended upon and torn apart by her group. Some would close shutters and doors if there were any, but most homes were in disrepair, wattle and daub structures, and easily broken into. If one of her kind happened upon an individual who was outside, such as a hunter camped in the woods, and that person was bitten but escaped, that person *might* be found later having turned, but it was not always the case.

Elizabeth sometimes tried to stop her people from devouring every living thing they attacked, but it was difficult. The better way to increase their numbers was to visit the grave pits. Nearly all the towns had them, even the deserted ones. When the plague hit, people first buried their dead in a church cemetery. As the death spread rapidly, the fear of this most painful death overtook religious morays, and the living only wanted the dead out of their homes. Mass graves, or death pits, were common. It was here Elizabeth often found followers either emerging from shallow graves or ransacking the village they had lived. Her kind did not eat each other, but a few would eat a corpse.

Elizabeth never commanded Nicola. Nicola would stay by her as much as possible, head hung down. Even during an attack, when they split up, Nicola would find her way back to Elizabeth's side. None of the others dared to approach Elizabeth or be so close. Again, it was not an intelligence working, but some instinct that they should follow Elizabeth. They had to keep a distance unless called for. And there was the sense among them if sense was the word, that Nicola could approach Elizabeth when others could not.

Some nights they wandered the countryside for hours and Elizabeth said not a word. At other times Elizabeth would talk to Nicola, who never answered, yet seemed to listen, even though Elizabeth sensed nothing in her mind. One particular night, caressing her ring, Elizabeth spoke at length to Nicola about Prospero, and his fine life in his fine castle and his fine mistress, and how wonderful it would be to find him in her presence, wouldn't it, Nicola?

But that was impossible, because the Prince had thrown them both out, along with Rose and Marie, and sealed the entranceway of the most hidden of entrances into the abbey, and Elizabeth had no idea how to get there. No, they would not see Prospero again.

Nicola said nothing but shuffled along behind Elizabeth. That was enough.

At times Elizabeth found stronger wood and hemp ropes in villages and made better splints for Nicola. If Elizabeth found yeast, she might try to ferment it and create alcohol, then she would bathe Nicola's legs in it. Something told her it helped cleanse the wounds. Elizabeth periodically replaced the linen. If Nicola was not getting better, at least she was not getting worse.

As to her other people, Elizabeth could not attend to them as well. Some would wander off, some would drop off from the pack, some would be torn apart during an attack on a boar or a bear. The energy drained quickly from their bodies. It was a constant search for food, from one prey to the other.

One night, Elizabeth slowly walked down a road, speaking aloud to Nicola. Elizabeth found a particularly hardy walking stick by the side of the road, made of olive wood. This must have been left here by a traveler. She used some rope she kept for such an occasion and tied the stick onto Nicola's right hand. Nicola stood patiently, staring downward.

Elizabeth stepped back. "Now try that." She began to back away from her.

Nicola shambled along, her face still hanging down, dragging the stick behind her.

Elizabeth shook her head. "How did you ever survive before I found you?" she asked aloud. "I wish you would learn to use a walking stick. But you can't, dear. Oh well." Elizabeth picked up another stick and banged it into the ground.

"This," she said. "Do this, Nicola. Do this," and as she spoke, she kept banging the stick into the ground.

Nicola stood silently before her, head hung as always. Then she slowly tamped the stick held in her own hand into the dirt and moved forward. Success!

Nicola struck the ground with her stick again and shambled forward.

"You are still my lady-in-waiting, Nicola," Elizabeth said. "Too bad we never found Marie or Rose. Then again, I was quite lucky to find you. You know–"

Nicola had stopped and pointed forward with her left arm.

Elizabeth leaned in and asked, "What is it?"

Head down, Nicola remained silent, still pointing.

There was a light fog about. The half-moon was only partially covered by clouds. In the moonlit fog were several large, hulking figures shambling toward them. Elizabeth reached out with her mind immediately.

*Ten of my kind. Mindless. Soldiers. No, Routiers. Paid mercenaries. This group came from southwestern France. They are part of the Archpriest's company! Mercenaries who were famed for storming castle walls. This group had been retained... by... by the Holy Roman Emperor and involved in an attack. They were separated from the main body of forces when they were attacked by fleshers.*

*The leader of this squadron.... his name... his name was Janosz. Janosz Ujvary. Towering height and a narrow waist, broad shoulders. But muscular. Much more so than any other of my kind that I've met before. There is a slight hitch in his gait. His shoulders are taller than my head!*

*And he is coming for me.*

***

STOP!

Elizabeth had to make a severe exertion to block the hulking soldier before her. Janosz Ujvary halted his walk, but his momentum carried him forward and he fell to the ground.

Elizabeth could not believe what had happened. Finding another like her, one with at least some sense of a mind–it was amazing. So much so she had been momentarily distracted to the point where she almost allowed her head to be ripped off, for that is what Janosz would have done. The man/flesher was on the ground, breathing heavily. The others following Janosz stopped. They were mindless, but they followed Janosz for some reason, attracted to him in the same unexplainable way as her followers.

Elizabeth tried speaking.

"Your name is Janosz?" she asked. "Janosz Ujvary?"

He did not respond but stayed on all fours.

Elizabeth's other followers were starting to catch up. Nicola crept close to her. Elizabeth motioned for her to stand back while she knelt next to Janosz. She reached into Janosz's mind.

"You have memories," she said. She sensed Janosz only understood her verbally. "You are from the German lands, yes? You fought with the Archpriest himself, Arnaud de Cervole. You were part of his band, the Great Company."

Janosz made no response.

*Irritating*, Elizabeth thought. *But perhaps not. Perhaps he–is he thinking?*

She read his mind further. This was a weak, fractured man, in no position to block my intrusion. He was bitten and the infection took him over until he died. But something primitive survived.

*I can read farther into his mind than he can recall. He is not aware of all these memories. He cannot process but he is... he is choosing not to answer me.*

How interesting. Elizabeth smiled. "I want to be your friend, Janosz. I want you to be my friend."

Still no response.

Elizabeth directed the other members of Janosz's party. They meandered like docile creatures toward her followers. Instinctively, they recognized Elizabeth's power.

She got on both knees, physically closer to Janosz. She could access more of his mind.

"You fought for Arnaud," she whispered. "You have a memory of that. Remember. You lead your men into battle. You were fighting for the Holy Roman Emperor against the Duke of Urbino... Ahh, but this Duke is a shrewd man. He had flesh eaters in his dominion. When you beat the Duke's army, the fleshers were released. In the confusion, you and your company were isolated from the main force. You wielded a great broadsword with both your hands the way some men use a rapier. Most of your squad fell. Not all turned at once, but you were overrun. But you slew all the creatures who attacked your party by slicing them into pieces with your broadsword.“

She paused. “And you were bitten.”

Janosz’s breathing had slowed, and his muscles were tightening. Good.

“The leader of the fleshers. There was an alpha. You recognized it. You smashed the pommel of your broadsword into its face, again and again, pounding it into a pulp. You knew the only way to kill the alpha was to destroy the brain. But the grip became bloodied, and your hand slipped, and you were bitten on the hand before you destroyed the alpha.“

She paused again, then read deeper still.

“Not all your company turned. Thirty out of one hundred survived. Some were bit but still not turned. You led your survivors back to Arnaud. And how were you treated? Like a monster. That’s what you are to them, a monster. They slaughtered your companions. You and a few others escaped him.”

Time for a calculated risk. Elizabeth touched the mercenary’s shoulder. Instantly her knowledge, and her control of the man, increased exponentially. She could have commanded his heart to stop. But that was far from what she wanted.

"Your mind is injured," she continued, "but you can comprehend mine. You are not a monster to me. You can sense that. You are now with your kind. We are forming a new great company, Janosz Ujvary. You and your men, they follow you because they sense you are different. My people follow me. Don't fight me. Come with me. We will seek out those who wronged us. We will have our revenge."

She leaned closer to his ear. "Would you like to be part of our new great company?"Janosz raised his head off the ground, not enough to meet her eyes.

His voice was a deep baritone. "Yes."

***

It was late spring. Elizabeth felt strong. At least, strong enough. She was still dying, of course. The tell-tale sign was the red hairs caught in her hands when she brushed herself. All her followers were dying. What kept them alive was a consuming urge, and the burning urge was to feed. The stronger could go for several days without eating, maybe two or even three weeks on rodents and animals.

The stronger ones tended to be quicker and could catch such prey. But the weaker ones–if they did not feed after three days, they would collapse and rot on the ground. There they would remain conscious for some time, but they would be too weak to move. Eventually, they would expire.

Elizabeth found herself constantly looking for food, for her people, and especially Nicola. Nicola appeared weak, yet she managed to sustain herself with small animals. She was not quick, but she had a knack for finding newborn birds and rodents. Sometimes she even ate plants. Nicola was very interesting, though quite mindless. Their problem was the food was scattered at best. The plague had hit these lands hard. Many had died. Survivors had often left. So they had to find pockets in villages where people were returning, or hiding, or for travelers through the region. It was a never-ending quest for food.

One evening Elizabeth found herself near a familiar place. She had been called, either of her own internal thoughts or something else. But why did not matter? What did matter was the question she needed answered.

Elizabeth stood at the top of the mausoleum looking down the stone stairwell. In the crypt below was the vampiress Ligeia. It had been months since she first came.

She recalled when she first arrived. It had been cooler with heavy driving rains from the end of summer to the early fall. Now it was a beautiful, cool spring evening.

Elizabeth took a deep breath, and the damp air invigorated her lungs. She descended.

Elizabeth glided down the stone steps, the ones she had struggled to crawl down not so long ago, and stopped by the cot she had spent so much time. Ligeia lay in it, weak, wearing a white gown covered in bloody phlegm.

She could converse with Ligeia's mind freely. It was effortless now. Yet seeing Ligeia's broken body caused her pause.

Elizabeth spoke aloud. "Why?"

"Why?" Ligeia uttered, struggling to speak. "Why did I make you? Or why am I being punished?"

Elizabeth thought for a moment.

"Both."

"The plague," Ligeia said weakly. "The Red Death. Some call it the Black Death." Ligeia rasped between breaths. "If you wished to die, I am sorry, my love. I've given you too much. It has mixed with the power of the Red Death. I should not have done what I did, but I had to. You understand?"

Elizabeth brushed back Ligeia's raven hair and nodded.

Ligeia said, "You are not one of my kind. You are more."

Ligeia gasped, clutching at her throat. Elizabeth watched her cough.

"There may be others, like you," Ligeia said.

"I have found them," Elizabeth added coldly.

"But even among them, you are different. A new kind," Ligeia said, coughing, then continuing. "I think–the ones who still follow the Christian god, they might call you a new—(cough)—a new 'Eve'."

Elizabeth knelt next to Ligeia and stroked her hair. Strands of it caught on her fingernails. She pulled up Ligeia's hand and noted the singular boniness of each digit.

"You are right," Elizabeth said. "I am not one of your kind. You've taken me and the Red Death has taken me. I have died, but I am not dead. I am something that has never existed."

Ligeia stared into her eyes.

"Do you want me to put you in your coffin?" Elizabeth asked.

"A village priest came and doused it with holy water," Ligeia said laughing. "Can you believe it?"

Her face grew dark. "It is no use to me. But it would not matter."

Elizabeth held up her forearm and asked, "Will feeding help you?".

"Our roles have reversed," Ligeia said, shaking her head. "I absorbed your sickness. I am dying. The vampire's death. We have a code–never give the lifeblood to one with the plague. And I violated that rule. And I am paying my price. And nothing you can do can reverse that." She coughed up more blood. "But you can do one thing. Will you kill me, Elizabeth?"

Elizabeth stared back vacantly.

Then she shook her head.

Ligeia feebly reached an arm across the cold marble floor, and two of her long, brittle fingernails shattered against the stone. Elizabeth could hear the sounds of her fingertips dragging against the cold marble floor, much as she'd once heard the sound of her husband–what was his name–banging his silverware against the banquet table.

"No," Elizabeth looked away. "I hate what I am. I hate what you've done to me. Yet I cannot do what you ask."

Elizabeth rose from her crouch and walked back up the stairs. There was a moaning behind her–louder than Elizabeth expected. She started to look behind but then stopped. Turning, Elizabeth gazed into the same cherub-lined mirror she had seen when she first entered this crept, barely alive, if alive at all, many, many months ago. She recalled the haggard, sopped visage that had greeted her back then.

Now the mirror only reflected the opposite side of the passage.

Elizabeth kept moving up the stone steps and out of the crypt. At the top, Janosz stood motionless, waiting. Some of the others stumbled through the dark, while others sat dumbfounded on the ground, awaiting some thought from Elizabeth to enter their head. But Janosz was not as feeble as the others. She could sense that he retained some faint memories, memories that even he could not recall. Not now. But he could develop the capacity to do so. She had resurrected a memory in him of who he had been. And he knew rudimentary speech.

Elizabeth had made clear, no one could enter the tomb. However, on the journey they passed a small village. Elizabeth had seen it before and found it deserted, but tonight a few fires were burning in some places. Not the village burning, but signs of life.

Her people were hungry. Their hunger was something she felt acutely. Elizabeth shut the door of the crypt.

"Janosz," she said. Her lieutenant stood firm. "Are you hungry?"

Janosz nodded.

Elizabeth smiled. “So am I.”

# Chapter 14

*What does Elizabeth want?*

***

Another night. Some time later. They had been fortunate, having come across a band of pilgrims journeying to view some cloth in Turin. Fortunate for Elizabeth, not so much for the pilgrims. Her people had attacked the caravan from all sides. It was not as organized as she wanted, but they had fed. Janosz had proven particularly useful. The sight of his six-foot-three frame storming out of the dark paralyzed people with fear. Janosz attacked with quick efficiency. His large hands could tear off a person's head, making an easy meal of the oh-so-desired brains. A few of the pilgrims were bitten and turned, becoming part of her pack. Her band was now well over one hundred strong. Still, it had been five days ago, and there was a renewed hunger.

There was no moon out tonight, and cumulus crowds blanketed the sky. They had wandered into an area that Elizabeth did not recognize, which was not unusual. Her memories faded in and out, and while more often she could remember things, sometimes she would be lost. Anyway, it did not matter, there was a thick fog about tonight that limited all visibility to a few feet.

Then, out in the distance, light. They collectively approached. Elizabeth saw it was what looked like an ale house with glass windows, lightly tinted, behind which she could see candles burning. It was unusual to find glass in anything but the finest of palaces and cathedrals, but here, in the middle of nowhere? The walls were made of stone with a wooden roof. Fairly well constructed. Elizabeth moved her people in a general circle around the building–she was getting better each night at controlling their direction, though the closer proximity she was to them, the greater her dominion. When her group had more or less surrounded it, she directed them to move in. They proceeded in. There had to be a few people in this place. Perhaps a few travelers stopped here to rest for the night. All the better.

Her people approached within a few steps of the tavern and stopped. She forced her will on them. They lurched and pawed at the air, but none would move closer toward the building.

Elizabeth turned to Janosz. "What's wrong?" she demanded.

Janosz held his hands in front of his face and looked away from the building. Elizabeth looked to Nicola who stood with her hood-covered head drooping toward the ground, motionless.

"Come with me," Elizabeth said.

Nicola made no reply. Elizabeth grabbed Nicola's arm, but Nicola pointed at the building, then shrank back.

Out of the corner of her eye, Elizabeth saw movement. This was intriguing.

Elizabeth let Nicola's arm go. "That's all right, Nicola," she said as she walked to the tavern. "You can all wait here. I'll only be a moment."

She went up to the entrance, a thick double-hung wooden door and pushed on it. The doors glided open easily, almost floating on air. Elizabeth stepped inside and surveyed the inside.Her first thoughts were, *Well, this is interesting*.

The tavern was much brighter than she had expected. The candles in the windows gave some light, but a great wooden chandelier hung in the middle of the main room which made it very easy to see. A large hearth on the left side burned bright. Purple tapestries surrounded the edges of each window. A stairway led to an upstairs area. The place was littered with chairs and stools, all pushed to the edges, save for one single bench set before a lone table. But what made the room even more interesting was its three inhabitants.

At the right, behind a bar, was a pretty blonde woman dressed in rags, washing the top of the long table. On the other side of the room, seated by the fire, was a brown-haired woman wearing a long white gown, sleeveless brown tunic, and a white wimple which covered her brown hair. At the far end of the room, a tall slender black-haired woman, sophisticatedly dressed in a red flowing gown adorned with rubies, seemed to be pacing mindlessly. Her black hair was wrapped in two plaits across the front of her head and trailed down the back.

The moment Elizabeth walked in, the black-haired woman turned to her and said, "Welcome, Elizabeth Malatesta, Princess of this land, yet not the princess."

The brown-haired woman, still tending the fire, sang, "Welcome, Elizabeth, wife of Prospero, alive and yet not alive."

The blonde one kept washing her table and chimed, "Welcome Elizabeth, Queen of the undead, though different than the undead."

Elizabeth paused. She reached into their minds but could not read a one.

*None of them look at me directly*, she thought. *They only show me their profile. And they conceal their eyes with their hair. The blonde is the youngest, the brown-haired one a little older, and the elegant woman is more mature. Or so is the appearance they offer me.*

But there was a distinct similarity in the features of their faces that was visible.

Elizabeth smirked.

"My wayward sisters," she said. "I had wondered when we might meet."

The raven-haired woman waived to the central table and commanded, "Sit. Share a drink with us." After a pause, she added, "Please."

"Why not?" Elizabeth said and strode over to the chair in the center of the room and sat.

The blonde-haired woman shuffled from behind the long table. Elizabeth saw she moved in a jerky, back-and-forth motion, and she had a humped back. The blonde brought Elizabeth a cup with a steaming broth and placed it on the table. She showed only the side of her face, her blonde curls carefully falling across her profile.

"For me?" Elizabeth asked. "What must I pay?"

The fair-haired woman replied, "Nothing, Elizabeth Malatesta. Drink to your health." The blonde retreated back to her long table.

Elizabeth laughed heartily and boldly proclaimed, "Elizabeth Malatesta is here!"

"To your health," the three sisters said in unison.

"Of course," Elizabeth said. She took the cup and drank it without hesitation. What harm could come of it? And if she were to perish–well, that would not be such a bad thing now, would it?" She took a sip.

"It is quite pleasant," she said. She took another sip. It was like human blood. Elizabeth was a flesh eater, not a vampire, but in consuming flesh she also absorbed blood, which was nourishing to her. This drink was like that but with a more filling sensation. Elizabeth said, "Quite satisfying," and drank the rest. When she had finished, Elizabeth put the cup down on the table and said, "Well, seeing as we all know each other, let's get to whatever business you have with me."

Elizabeth began to twist her hair in her hand, then added somberly "But you three are mistaken about me. Elizabeth Malatesta is dead. I am something else."

"Really?" the blonde asked.

"Really?" repeated the black-haired woman.

"Really?" echoed the brown-haired woman by the fire.

"You wander the fog-drenched forests at night, struggling to survive," the blonde said, pointing an accusing finger at Elizabeth.

"You seek rats and humans for food," the brown-haired one cackled.

"You do this while Prospero feasts atop Mount Pirchiriano, living in luxury, while he thinks he keeps the Red Death at bay," the raven-haired one declared. "Even now he prepares for a great feast to celebrate his life, a masquerade that celebrates his triumph over the Red Death."

Elizabeth looked at her hand which held a fistful of red hair. She relaxed her fingers and watched her strands fall to the floor. Then she asked, "What care of that is mine?"

"Was he not the cause of Elizabeth's misfortune?" asked the blonde.

“Was Prospero not the instrument of Elizabeth’s misery?” the brown-haired one chimed.

“Is there not another who has wrongfully taken Elizabeth’s rightful place in the Abbey?” queried the raven-haired one.

“When he mocks the Red Death, he mocks you,” said the brown-haired one.

“He makes merry with many and laughs at death,” the blonde one said.

“You chose to accept his mockery of you,” the black-haired one said.

Elizabeth smiled slyly and looked at a candle in the window. She could picture Prince Prospero and the feast he was having. Wine, dancing, beauty, jongleurs, jugglers, tellers of tales, musicians, more dancing, totally sealed in their castle, and lacking any concern or fear for the outside.

Elizabeth momentarily lost track of where she was, but then she became aware another drink had been placed in front of her. She picked it up and drank more. Then the black-haired woman stood by the table and whispered into her ear.

“Why shouldn’t Elizabeth Malatesta return to her kingdom?”

“Why should she?” Elizabeth asked.

"Because she wants to," the blonde said. She was beside Elizabeth's other ear.

The brown-haired one by the fire said, "Because *Sacra di San Michele* is filled with warm bodies."

"Think of it" whispered the well-dressed woman with the plaited black hair. "An Abbey filled with one thousand bodies, healthy, well fed, and nourished."

In her mind, Elizabeth saw the revelers, dancing in the halls of the abbey (whether the image was of her own creation or implanted there, she could not tell). These were not thin and weak survivors in some desolate hovel, all skin and bones and emaciated. These were people who laughed while the plague ravaged outside their compound. She could smell their perfumed scent, see their well-fed mouths laughing gaily, and hear their blood throbbing through their bodies turning on the dance floor.

"A most pleasant image," Elizabeth said. "But not all of Elizabeth's memories have returned."

"The ones she needs to have," said the black-haired woman. "That which is never gone needs only to be reawakened." A hand touched Elizabeth's forehead.

Suddenly, Elizabeth could see outside the tavern, looking on as she had before. Then she was racing through the woods as if she was being carried by some magical carpet, but incredibly fast. The thick forest was a blur. Yet as quickly as she moved, she was aware of where each of these places were, and how they were connected. It was too fast to process but she did remember it. She was still in the tavern, Elizabeth was sure of it, but her mind had flown.

Then she was standing outside a heavily bolted iron door at the base of *Sacra di San Michele.*

"The Abbey is sealed," she said. "The exterior paths are watched. There is no way to enter."

Though she seemed to be standing before the very door where she had stood so long ago heard the black-haired one's voice say," Save for here."

Elizabeth could move. She touched the metal door and sensed its thickness. Her tactile sense felt three great crossbars of iron going across, and the bolts which had been welded and hammered to hold the bars in place, sealing the portal.

"This is impenetrable," she said.

Elizabeth found herself seated at the same table as before, but still out in the woods, a few yards from the same door. Two of the sisters were to each side of her, while the third, the brown-haired one, tended a fire a short way off, stirring a steaming cauldron.

“Tis impenetrable, she says” the brown-haired one chirped.

“Tis a barrier,” said the blonde.

“Tis nothing that is impenetrable,” said the black-haired one, “if one knows *how* to pierce the barrier.”

Elizabeth watched the brown-haired take a pair of tongs which held a long glass tube, and dip the tube into the cauldron. When she pulled it out it contained a red steaming liquid. The brown one cackled as she waddled over to the table.

Elizabeth felt the black-haired woman (who seemed to be the greater of the three) pull her back, and they both glided with the tubes away from the table. Three iron bolts stood upright on the table. The blonde woman raised her finger in the air and motioned to watch while she held a copper bucket in the other. Reaching into the bucket, she poured a dark gold liquid into a smaller glass container. The brown-haired woman carried the glassine container and set it on the table, then handed a brush to her black-haired sister. The black-haired sister dipped the brush into the container and swirled it, then took it out and swabbed the three bolts on the table. The night air filled with a loud hiss. Smoke engulfed the room. Elizabeth saw the liquid dissolving the bolts.

*It is as if it were alive,* she thought. While the metal burned there was an odor of sulfur and molten iron, as if being smelt in a giant kiln. More smoke–no, she thought, *it is steam*–engulfed them all. Elizabeth pawed at the gas surrounding her.

A deafening wind howled in her ears.

The steam cleared.

There were three holes in the table where the pins had been. A metallic residue encircled the holes.

"They've been melted," Elizabeth said breathlessly.

Then she was back in the tavern. It was dark, with only a small fire burning in the hearth.

The women were gone.

Where the table had been, was a small pile of white powdered ash. And a few feet away, a closed wooden chest lay on the floor. Elizabeth walked over to the chest and pulled it open.

She stared at the contents for some time, processing what she saw.

Then she knew.

She would be calling on Prospero after all.

# CHAPTER 15

## *WARNINGS*

***

*It is so damn cool in here, even at this time of year,* Clarinda Corrato thought as she tightened a shawl around her shoulders. Carrying a torch, she walked along this half-buried subterranean passageway in the castle as she had often done. This way was seldom used. It had been dug into the granite bedrock long ago.

It was very quiet. Deathly so. Why did she brave the coolness and the darkness down here? Very few people knew of this place. Prince Prospero had forbidden any to walk down here since the day he had cast out Elizabeth and her ladies-in-waiting. *Of course, it had been the right thing to do,* Clarinda had told herself, over and over again.

Elizabeth was sick.

Elizabeth had coughed up blood.

She had the most deadly form of the great mortality. The girls would have followed shortly. Surely their bodies lay rotting somewhere outside the Abbey's sealed walls, probably no more than a few feet away. Was it wrong for the healthy to protect their lives?

Clarinda Corrato reached the chamber at the end of the tunnel as she had done before. She raised the torch over *that* metal gate. The bolt heads had been driven so deep they were flush with the door. She ran her hand over the boltheads. Each one was cold and firm without any trace of looseness. Shaking her head, she turned and began walking back, muttering, "I hate it down here."

"Then why do you come so often?" came a voice from the far side of the chamber.

Clarinda flashed her torch to the side and saw an elderly woman sitting on the ground. She wore a full body cloak with the hood down, revealing a great shock of white hair that covered most of the woman's face, except for where a sharp nose jutted out.

"Who are you?" Clarinda asked, her voice trembling.

"One you have no need to fear," the woman replied.

Clarinda waved the torch back and forth. The chamber seemed otherwise empty, but she could not see into all the shadows. Still, she was Prospero's woman.

"You watch me then?" Clarinda asked.

The woman was throwing sticks and colored stones onto a pile of sand, then picking them up with one hand, rubbing them between her palms, and dropping them again. As she did, she said, "You come here more frequently."

It was true. Clarinda had vowed never to come here again, not since that day so long ago. For the first and second months, she kept the promise to herself. She was Prospero's woman, the princess of the Abbey. Even if Prospero may have had a dalliance with another woman or two, she could overlook it. Her authority remained strong. But in the third month, she had first come down here. Why she could not say, but she was drawn here. Something about the doors. They were welded shut and the passage was dug right into the bedrock of Mount Pirchiriano, the mountain *Sacra di San Michele* Abbey was located atop. It would take a hundred men with iron tools months to tunnel through, and they would be far from silent. No, the inhabitants of the Abbey were secure. Another month went by and she came down and found everything as before. And so another month, and another. By her count, almost twelve months had gone by.

"You are troubled, are you not?" asked the woman, still playing with her sticks and stones.

Clarinda replied, "Why should I be? I am Prince Prospero's woman."

"You are," said the figure. "For the moment."

"Who are you?" Clarinda asked. "An oracle? There are already two oracles in this castle."

"Yes, that is true," the figure said. "But there was the old monk who you confided in and secretly brought into these walls. He died in the fourth month of confinement."

Clarinda put her hand to her heart at the words.

"How did you know that?" Clarinda asked. "And what do you want?"

The woman dropped her sticks and stones and then used a narrow, bony finger to stir them around as she spoke.

"You are both good and bad, Clarinda," the woman replied. "As are most. But in your life, you respected and honored the fates. Now the fates reach out to you."

Clarinda stood in her spot, feeling both fearful and angry.

The woman continued. "The Prince prepares a great masquerade ball, does he not? And you feel trepidation at it, do you not? You feel unease at about who revealed the plans for the Great Hall, do you not? That is why you come to this place more and more. Every day since he announced the ball."

Clarinda shrugged her shoulders and tried to sound haughty by saying, "Life is better inside these walls than without them. Or would you like to be sent away?"

But the hag's words were true. Clarinda, she had concerns over the dream Prospero had, or more particularly, the appearance of Nicole, Rose, and Marie in the dream.

"The Prince was not told to build his room," the woman said. "He was shown what he wanted."

Clarinda felt a shiver throughout. She also recalled the old stories of how Elizabeth had been involved in the black arts.

The woman stopped with the sticks and pressed a hand to the ground. "The Prince makes a mockery of the fates with his blasphemous charade. He makes a bold jest in the face of the Red Death. The Red Death comes, he will not see its face, nor can he hide from it. Same as you. But you, Clarinda," the woman paused, "you may *run* from it."

Clarinda's anger suddenly overtook her fear and she said, "You should not be down here!"

The woman picked up the stones in both hands and clasped them tight.

"Remember, Clarinda, the fates seldom make a second gift of a person's life."

Clarinda began to storm toward the woman and said, "I will have you thrown from the eastern ramparts of this Abbey!"

The air was broken with the sound of the ringing of a great clock striking the hour, like a gong. Clarinda shuddered at the musical note which reverberated against all the walls of the corridor.

The door to the outside!

Clarinda turned and ran to it.

The door stood silent, holding firm.

Clarinda waited several moments, listening intently.

Nothing.

She turned. The woman was gone. Of course.

Clarinda ran out of the chamber.

***

The town of Avigliana was almost empty, save for a few souls secreted away. Those few who were alive seldom went far from whatever shelter they could find but crept out during the day only to forage for food. There was no moon. An old woman with a black overcoat and a shock of white hair and a crooked nose walked through Avigliana, a stick in hand. She turned around a waddle and daub house and continued into what was once a vibrant village square. There she found two other white-haired women, dressed in rags, standing by a small cauldron suspended over fire. The pot was smoking heavily. One of the women stayed by the fire and fed it while the other reached into satchels she carried around her waist and dropped into the pot equal mixes of cheese, bread, and live vermin. One might've thought there was a familial resemblance between the three women if one was there to see them.

The two women by the fire took no notice of the woman approaching, but once the woman arrived, the one tending the fire asked, "And what was the response, sister?"

The woman with the walking stick answered, "As you expected, my sister." The woman pulled the hood off her head. "She rejects our intervention."

The woman stirring the pot said, "But we have done what we were obligated to do."

The woman who had removed her hood said, "Indeed we have."

The woman feeding the cauldron said, "Then I am most happy, sister. Most happy."

The smoke emanating from the kettle grew thicker, engulfing the women.

And then they were gone.

# CHAPTER 16

*Prince Prospero's Dream Rooms. Several days later. Early in the evening.*

*Sacra di San Michele.*

***

FANTASTIC COLORS TWIRLED AROUND Clarinda's face as the celebrants whirled and turned with ever-increasing revelry, giving in to the beat rising in the chamber. The music from the orchestra whistled in her ears. A person with lesser focus would have found themselves swept up in the spectacle. But Clarinda remained steadfast and focused on maintaining the visible yet reserved smile befitting the Lady of the castle. She moved through the assembly on Prospero's arms with Giancarlo and several other guards trailing.

And what an assembly it was. Every corner of the grand hall was filled with friends and fiends bedecked in wild colors. Various goblins and ghouls, prostitutes and patrons, saints and sinners reveled among ice-sculptured fish sitting in vast bowls of wine. Austerity was not the word that evening. The more garish, the more fanciful the costume, the better. Harlequin masks and mufti linens which clung close to the body were worn by dancers who lined the edge of the chambers (except for the last one, but we shall discuss that shortly). These dancers, who had been strictly prescribed by Prince Prospero, danced solely with themselves, constantly forming an arabesque pose and twirling on one foot, then to the other foot, switching and twisting in the opposite direction.

Clarinda thought the Prince seemed in a particularly sagacious mood tonight as he and walked through the throng. They started in the blue room. The relatively long length and narrow width of the chamber packed in the crowd, which the Prince enjoyed. He had been planning this fete for some time and had this hall built under a shroud of mystery. Various workers labored on different stages so only he knew what the exact configuration would be.

It was a strange great hall, consisting of seven suites, all in the interior of the castle, running the full length of the Abbey from the east end to the west. There was but one main point of egress and ingress, a large set of double-hung, solid oak doors at the far eastern end of the hall. Two narrow corridors lined the outside of the hall's walls for servants to come and go unobserved.

Prince Prospero had spent some months having this monstrosity constructed within the abbey. It gave the workers in the Abbey something to do (most craftsmen were not among the couple's closest friends, but it was practical to have some skilled workers amongst the population). What was particularly interesting was the layout of the rooms within the hall. Each chamber was built at an angle to the other so that after one walked the length of the room, one would take a sharp turn to enter the next room. One could only see the room one was in. No one could see across the length of the chamber, so the entire single color of the room dominated. Clarinda thought the optical illusion gave people a sense of unease. Prospero seemed to enjoy giving his friends this sense.

"You seem happy," she said over the din.

Prospero threw his head back, laughed, and took a great goblet of wine to his lips.

"Why shouldn't we be? There is none in our lands who is not here who does not wish they were here. And there is none more fortunate than you, Clarinda, for being here." He gave her a drunken kiss on the lips.

None of the rooms opened to the outside, save for the easternmost chamber. The blue room, which had the aforementioned doorway on its eastern end, went to the other parts of the Abbey. Each room was bathed in one color, generated in two ways. First, each room had a lush carpet across the entire floor and rich silken tapestries hung on its walls. Second, in the middle of the right and to left wall of each chamber, a stained-glass window stood which burned a flame, based on a tripod that lay in the servant's corridors running along the sides of both rooms, and these two lights on each side of the chamber gave each apartment its light. The servants had been commanded to maintain the fires, but never be seen doing so, upon pain of being banished from the Abbey. And here, those condemned to banishment by the Prince's justice were tossed from the upper ramparts as everyone knew from the fate of four unfortunates who had not pleased the Prince on a particularly bad day for him.

Among the rooms, blue was the first, as noted. Here all the food and drink was not only stored, but prepared so the room could be sealed shut and no one would leave after dusk.

Clarinda and Prince Prospero made their way along to the next room, bathed in purple light, where a set of musicians played, and through that to the next, the green room. Often the revelers could not see the Prince and his beloved until they were upon them, and then the people would nervously part and beg the Prince's forgiveness. The couple dodged a group of drunken revelers engaged in a mock pantomime, encircling a nubile woman totally nude but for brown and red body paint while chanting the child's rhyme "Ring around the Rosie." As Clarinda went past, the entire group fell as one to the ground, while the naked woman laughed and threw rose petals upon them.

At the corner angle where the chamber branched off to the orange room, Prince Prospero said to Clarinda, "Watch what I have set up for you."

In the orange chamber, two high-backed chairs bedecked in jewels sat upon a dais which took two steps to reach. Though there was nourishment in every room, a particularly bountiful cornucopia of food and drink was set on long tables throughout the orange room. A small group of musicians played in the far corner.

"We will come back to this," Prince Prospero said, "but let me show you the rest."

"Why Prospero," Clarinda said, "This seems to be a wonderful place right here. Let's eat and drink with our friends. I like this room."

"Yes, but you must see the entire structure," Prospero said.

They proceeded onward, through the fifth room, the white room, which had the most space for dancing, and into the sixth room, the violet room. (For those of you asking the difference between purple and violet, you must imagine purple being the redder, more saturated color, while violet is lighter and closer to blue). Each room was filled with masked revelers making merry, while a few servants darted almost unseen like field mice, to maintain the flow of food and drink.

This violet room was the second to the last room in the chain heading west. The color and dim light rolled in with the various revelers, and a set of musicians played on a stage set up in the corner of the room. In the middle, on another elevated platform, dancers swayed to the music. Unlike in the other rooms, fewer servants appeared. Wine spouted from bronze, naked cherubs adorning two large fountains, one at the entrance and one at the exit to the final room.

The courtiers seemed even more intoxicated with the euphoric atmosphere than in the previous chambers as if something had drawn out the most stout and sagacious, but they gravitated away from the the black room.

Clarinda walked into the violet room slowly but found herself bending and swaying under and around persons. For the most part, the revelers parted. A young courtier probably similar in age to Prospero, grabbed her arms as if to dance, but she smiled coyly and slithered out of his hands, guiding another girl into her place. The Prince's face showed anger, and as they moved along, Clarinda saw Giancarlo grab the young man by the shoulders. More drunken dancers swirled by, blocking Clarinda's view.

The final room was unlike the others, and even Prospero paused. Black tapestries covered the walls and a thick, velvet carpet hit the floor. If the lighting in the other rooms was garish, here it was strangely frightening. There was only one tripod burning behind the glass near the entrance. The glass was tinged red so the flickering flames produced the effect of blood continuously splashing across the walls and floors. Between the darkness and the tapestries, Clarinda could not make out the dimensions of the room, though the location of the single light suggested it was a large diamond shape. The black room was empty of revelers, and indeed, of any entertainment. Where the other rooms opened to yet another room, the black one dead-ended, with a large black wall, barren save for a tall, single ebony mechanical clock resting against the far end of the room. What one did hear most distinctly was the click-clack of the great timepiece's balance wheel grinding along.

As Prospero and Clarinda approached the timepiece, the clip of the balance wheel seemed to grow louder, and the music from the other chambers grew more faint.

"My Prince," Clarinda said, "If you wanted to create a sense of dread that would keep people out, you have succeeded." She forced her voice to be casual and relaxed.

"I built this place from the dreams I had," the Prince said, staring at the clock. "A recurrent dream. Each night I dreamt of this place. I was always guided by three guides. Sometimes three women. Sometimes three young boys. Once it was even–"

He was about to mention Nicola, Rose, and Marie, but caught himself.

"What?" Clarinda asked, feeling more anxious..

Prospero said, "One thing. In my dreams, I never saw this clock. I don't even know how it got here."

He turned to Clarinda and shrugged. “One of my carpenters must have been inspired to build it.”

“Let’s leave here,” Clarinda said.

She expected the Prince to argue, but he silently turned and escorted her out of the chamber.

# CHAPTER 17

*The approach of the Red Death*

***

WHILE PROSPERO AND CLARINDA toured his dream room, Elizabeth and her followers were outside the Abbey. By the iron door through which Elizabeth and her ladies-in-waiting had been thrown out of a year before. Or perhaps it had been two years.

Their journey had taken weeks, mostly at night, with undead animals carrying some of what they needed (an insight given to her by the three sisters). Some who started the journey did not complete it, but others had joined them. Elizabeth only vaguely remembered the way, but each time she came to a turn in the road, or where paths crossed, or even upon open fields, a memory came back to her (perhaps with intervention from the three sisters). Travelling up the mountain had been draining, but Elizabeth was determined. She had used her mind force to guide a good size group (over one hundred strong, though for some reason Elizabeth has lost the ability to count) up the winding paths leading to *Sacra di San Michele*. Most she now held back under the cover of trees. Though out of her sight, they were in close enough proximity to her, she could control them. Now she stood at the base of the Abbey, her followers with her, Nicole beside her. The night was cool, but not uncomfortably so, and the sky was clear.

Elizabeth wrapped her arms around Nicola's shoulders and asked, "Do you remember this Nicola? Do you remember what happened here? Do you remember how we were tossed from this place like garbage, excrement? You and I, and Rose and Marie?"

Nicola made no acknowledgement, but she swayed back and forth.

"You do remember," Elizabeth stated. "Even though you are mindless–you remember something."

In and around this area were several skeletons and partially decomposed bodies. Elizabeth noted them with a sneer. The stream running nearby–the one Nastagio's body had been thrown into nearly a year ago–carried the waste from the Abbey off of the mountain. This was also the base of one of the highest spots in the Abbey, the place where Prince Prospero would toss a body from the ramparts in full view of many inside.

"I can imagine there are a few revelers inside who regret being sealed in with someone like Prospero," Elizabeth said quietly to Nicola. "I am sure he had to make some examples to reinforce how one unwise it would be to express a desire to leave."

Just beyond the stream burned a small fire. Here Elizabeth had erected a firm spit on which hung a metal bucket holding water and several wide-mouth glassine bottles and decanters. A bubbling mixture with a strong sulfur odor percolated in each bottle.

Through the trees, she scanned the high walls of *Sacra di San Michele*. The spot was a promontory that jutted out from Mount Pirchiriano over the Susa Valley. Within this overgrowth of trees, this area was not particularly visible from the Abbey, and smoke from a small fire could easily be mistaken for the mists that often curled around the mountain when a warm day was followed by a cool night. Still, there was risk.

She led Nicola to the fire, where the massive Janosz, and a pair of Janosz's other men who had proved well maintained and who could follow simple commands, branches and stoking the flames.

The bottles in the bucket hanging over the fire were emitting smoke with the strong odor that included sulfur and others that burned the nose.

"Hurry," Elizabeth whispered. Wearing a set of thick leather gloves and using the set of iron tongs given her by the sisters, she grasped a wide mouthed decanter and lifted it out of the bucket as the brown-haired witch had shown her. The liquid inside was a bubbling, thick red-orange mixture. Still holding the bottle in the tongs, she carried this container across the stream to the iron doorway.

An intricate structure had been erected in front of the door. About eight feet above the ground was a large glass container which ran a network of spindly glass tubes on sticks. The container was wide, and the tubes narrowed into smaller tips that were positioned to end atop each bolt protruding from the iron door. A small wooden chest was set next to this. Elizabeth stepped up on the box and using the tongs, emptied the contents of the glass decanter into the basin. Steam burst up.

The reddish-orange mixture snaked its way from the container and through the tubes.

"More," Elizabeth said. She tossed the empty glass bottle aside and hurried back to the fire. She repeated her movements as before. Again. And again. On the fourth trip, as she poured the liquid, she saw the first batch had reached the end of the tubes and dripped onto the bolts. It reminded Elizabeth of the smell of molten iron being made in a blast furnace. She had watched one as a youth in her father's kingdom. Another random memory which came to her.

The liquid bubbled and ate into the iron with a hiss, smoldered, and left a hole where a bolt had been. This happened at several spots on the doors.

Elizabeth smiled. "It does work," she said quietly. She went back to get more of the mixture.

The wayward sisters had been most generous in their gifts. It would be impolite not to use them.

***

After some time, many of the bolts had dissolved. Elizabeth had the tubes and the structures holding them pulled away. She also had multiple bags of sand, carried up the mountain path on the backs of packmules, thown down in front of the door, and then covered with blankets. Janosz and his two men, under Elizabeth's direction, wedged tree branches with sharpened ends into the door. Along the edges, on the sides, underneath. They broke several tree branches, testing the door. It would not yield. Not at first. But then, Janosz, by himself, using both his immense shoulders, wedged a branch between the top of the iron and the stone, and Elizabeth saw a slight movement.

"There," Elizabeth said. "Right there, Janosz. Right there." She went up to him and changed the grip he was holding the branch with.

"Try now," she said.

Janosz pushed again. This time the door moved more. Elizabeth directed the other two to wedge smaller sharper branches into the sides of the entryway.

After several more attempts, a part of the door shifted, spreading a cloud of dust.

"Just a little more my friends," Elizabeth said.

They pushed further until Elizabeth heard the hinges snapping and the door pulling from the crossbars. She moved Janosz and the others back.

The door fell quickly and hit the ground with a thud. The sand and blankets had softened the fall, but there was still vibration.

"Damn," Elizabeth muttered. "We should have cushioned that better Nicola. But if the party is as garish as expected, a little extra noise won't be noticed. Either way, this is no time to stop.

Elizabeth had a sudden inspiration.

"Nicola," she said, "look around. Feel the air. This is the same place, and the same time of year, we were turned out from *Sacra di San Michele*. Last year. Or perhaps the year before." Nicola's head bent up and down slightly. Elizabeth hugged Nicola. "Tonight Prince Prospero and Clarinda are holding a gay soiree. Won't they be happy to see us!"

# Chapter 18

*The Red Death arrives*

***

Farther into the castle, Prospero clapped from his makeshift "throne" on the dais in the orange room. The arabesque dancers performed a synchronized rhythmic ballet. They jumped and writhed and rolled while carrying long streamers attached to canes which the dancers never stopped waiving. Clarinda was impressed with the athletic display. But then–

"Did you hear that?" she asked.

"Wonderful," the Prince said. "This is entertainment, is it not?" Perhaps he had not heard her. It was loud in the chamber.

"I thought I heard something," Clarinda said.

"There is much to hear!" said the Prince smugly.

"No, it was like something large had fallen," Clarinda said. "Didn't you feel a slight tremor under foot?"

Prince Prospero tapped her hand and said, "One of the servants dropped a vat of stew." He leaned into her and said, "Do not ruin this night, my dear. The mountain often groans at night." Then he stood and gestured throughout the room, saying, "Is this not wonderful?"

The crowd around him, a cavalcade of masked figures, greeted him with an enthusiastic, "Yes, Prince Prospero!"

Clarinda cast her eyes down and said, "My lord, this is most impressive."

"You were the one who gave me the strength to do what was right when I was weak," Prospero said. "And look at us. You were right. All this is here because of you."

Clarinda felt pain in her stomach at these words.

Prospero took Clarinda's leave and nodded to the ever-present Giancarlo, who followed the Prince.

***

Prospero wandered among his guests, shaking hands, accepting hugs, and kissing the hands of lithe women who kneeled in front of him. Giancarlo, along with a few of his guards, always stood a few feet behind. Prospero had ordered that the guards all wore their most resplendent uniforms, save for a domino mask on the face. Each guard wore a different mask. Prospero made his way to the blue room and took a great mug of wine from a passing servant but before he drank, a voice yelled above the cacophony.

"A toast! A toast to our savior and redeemer, Prince Prospero!"

A wild chant of appreciation erupted from the crowd.

Prospero raised his mug high and said, "My friends, through good fortune and careful detail, we are alive and healthy within these walls. Outside the great mortality rages. Outside is pestilence, desolation, and the scent of death is everywhere. In here there is food, drink, solidarity, and fellowship. No matter what happens outside, no matter how long it takes, we know we shall remain here until the Red Death passes."

Another round of supportive cries erupted, and Prospero gulped a large swig of wine. *Elderberry. Not bad*, he thought. He was halfway through another gulp when he saw an image that made him gag.

A figure had appeared at the edge of the blue room, where it turned into purple. A figure dressed in a black burial gown, a cloak wrapped close to the head, and long sleeves ending in a wide swath on the floor so no flesh was exposed. It was encased in a white mask molded in the form of a human face. The cloak's pitch black color contrasted starkly with the mask's whiteness, and the entire outfit seemed to scream defiance amidst the colorful sea of masqueraders. But that wasn't the most abhorrent part. The white mask and the black cloak were dabbed with blood-red streaks.

The blue room had grown silent, save for Prospero's choking on his drink. He called out, "You there! Who are you?"

The crowd parted to open a space directly between Prospero and the figure. The death mummer was facing the purple room, but upon being called, it turned to Prospero, raised a white gloved hand, and slowly wagged a finger back and forth.

Prospero, as the rest of the assembly, stood transfixed in place.

"You mock the Red Death!" Prospero said.

The figure turned and disappeared around the edge, entering into the purple room.

For a moment, no one said anything. Oh, there was still music emanating from the rooms farther west where there were those who could not see what has happening, but everyone in the blue room could hear the voices in the purple suddenly go silent, the music ceasing.

Prospero saw faces hidden by masks all around him. But these masks left the eyes exposed. In those eyes, he saw fear. And something else. The great Prospero had been challenged, and Propsero had not met the request. This insult gave him intense outrage which overwhelmed his fears.

Propsero gathered his courage and pulled Giancarlo close to him.

"Give me a dagger!" he commanded Giancarlo, who complied. Prospero ordered, "Seize that person!" The Prince stormed off in pursuit.

Giancarlo waived his hand, and several guards dressed as revelers fell in after him.

The phantom walked unimpeded through the purple room, then the green room, and still continued. At the phantom's appearance, each room went from a loud and raucous party to a deathly quiet chamber. Dancing and music immediately stopped, and the most mad of revelers parted before the approaching, shrouded figure.

Clarinda watched from her chair as the figure passed by. The entire chamber was silent, save for the sounds of hushed breathing. The mummer paused for a moment and glanced at the dais. It looked right at her! Then it continued into the white room, and onto the violet room.

When Prospero, Giancarlo, and the others pursued a few seconds later, Clarinda called out for Prospero to wait, but he ignored her, instead ordering people to apprehend the figure.

None in the chamber noticed the ragged figures filling into the servant corridors running parallel to the hall. If they had noticed, they would have seen the figures were bloodied and ravenous.

***

Prospero burst into the violet room, Giancarlo and guards trailing a few feet behind him. The suddenly not-so-gay revelers parted to make a straight path down the center of the room leading to the tall, gaunt figure. The mummer stood at the entry to the black room, which was empty save for the ebony clock. Her back was to them, but then the figure's head slowly turned its left shoulder. Though the blood-streaked face mask was without eyeholes, the figure gazed directly at Prospero. Then the face turned away, and the phantom walked into the black room, where it disappeared among the darkness.

***

Elizabeth entered the final black room, dominated by its only regular occupant, the great black clock.

Only?

She laughed to herself as she heard the scuffling of feet behind the walls. Mentally she held her people in check. It was not easy. Their blood lust was strong, and with roughly a thousand hale and hearty, well-nourished bodies in the area–well, it took all her command to hold them at bay. But she had to. Perhaps it was vanity. But she had to do one thing first.

# Chapter 19

*Masks of Death*

***

For a moment, Prince Prospero hesitated. But lest you think he was alone, know that none moved in the any of the apartments. The majority had crowded into the white and violet rooms behind to watch the parade unfold, though a few clustered as far away as possible, in the blue room. They did not seem to notice the masked servants shambling along the outside hallways. The only sound one could hear was the clicking of the of the ebony clock, its balance wheels grinding back and forth, which could be heard throughout all seven apartments.

Anger overcame Prospero's fear. He rushed across the violet room and launched himself into the black one, arching his arm back with a knife drawn. The figure waited until Prospero was within a few feet, then it turned to face him.

Prospero stopped, and lowered his knife. "Who are you?" he asked through suddenly labored breathing.

Now, so very close to the phantom, Prospero saw the mask was actually not white, but translucent around the eyeholes. There *were* eyes behind the mask. Familiear eyes.

Prospero again pulled his dagger back and readied to strike. "Who are you?" he repeated.

The face mask fell to the side without the mummer even touching it.

Prospero stared into an ivory countenance. Like the mask, it was smeared with streaks of blood.

"Don't you recognize your own wife, Prospero?" Elizabeth asked.

***

All the strength within the Prince flowed from him. The dagger dropped harmlessly from his hands onto the black carpet.

Elizabeth took one step toward him, entering his thoughts.

*You so feared the Black Death, Prospero*, her voice said inside his mind. *But you forgot about the Red Death.*

Her former husband–former? They had not divorced. Regardless, Prospero stood shaking underneath his costumed robe.

Again, inside his mind, she said, *Are you leaking, Prospero? Your piss is ruining this luxurious black carpet.*

Elizabeth took another step forward, wrapped him in a tight embrace, and kissed him forcefully on the lips. Prospero could not look away from her gaze, and he saw her iris's turn from blue to burnt orange. He could hear his blood heating up in his bod like boiling water.

Strength and will had departed Prospero, but the Prince could still feel sensations, and what he felt now were thousands of tiny needles. Not from without, but within! His body shuddered uncontrollably.

Elizabeth released him from her embrace, then reached down for the fallen mask. Prospero fell to his knees and bent over, wrapping his arms around his stomach. She had thought she would feel more triumph by now. Instead, as she stared down at her former husband, she felt only disgust.

"Just die, Prospero."

Prince Prospero Malatesta fell face forward onto the lush black carpet. His eyes collapsed on the black carpet, staring vacantly at the purple flames in the next room. Boils and sores had burst all over his once beautiful face and body. His blond hair was blood-soaked.

Another power revealed to her by the sisters.

“I am the Red Death,” Elizabeth said quietly. It was not as satisfying as she had hoped. But as she stood over Prospero’s motionless corpse, a new wave of triumph washed over her. She threw her head back and yelled, “And the Red Death conquers all!”

As the sentence left her lips, the chimes of the ebony clock sprung. Elizabeth’s head felt a pain, as controlling her people caused her mental fatigue.

“It’s almost done,” she said quielty.

Then she released her followers. And she felt relief.

The fleshers were free to feed however they wished, save for two of the revelers.

***

*Well, dear reader, if you have travelled with us this far, you can probably imagine the next scene. I must warn you, it is not for the faint of heart.*

*Do you wish me to continue? Wouldn't you prefer a pause?*

*As you wish.*

*Then listen well.*

# Chapter 20

*The Princess of the Abbey. Part II.*

***

THE SMASHING GLASS ANNOUNCED the beings were coming in from the two servant corridors that ran parallel to all seven apartments in the chamber. The fleshers numbered just over one hundred fifty, and the guests were close to a thousand. Perhaps a battle seasoned group, trained to face such an enemy and with sufficient warning to raise a defensive fortification, might have been able to repel the invaders. But it was just conjecture. Those were costumed pantomimists, awash in wines and grogs, trapped in a long, narrow enclosure, with fleshers streaming from both sides. Recall there was but one way to escape, and that was through a large door at the east end of the blue room, which had been locked. In that blue room, several servants were stunned when the fleshers poured in and turned them into the feast. A handful of hearty souls made it to the doors of the blue room but Elizabeth had stationed Janosz and his men there.

A man and a woman dressed in fine white linens grabbed silver candlesticks and ran up in a fear filled rage at Janosz. He grabbed them both by the throat, one hand each, and crushed their necks, then tossed their bodies to the side while blood splattered on him.

In the purple room, the fleshers burst in upon a set of musicians who were overtaken in their chairs. In the green room, the nude women who had been dancing in circles found their painted and perfumed bodies gave a particularly strong scent that attracted the attackers. The fleshers ate and tore and gorged themselves on the revelers who were surrounded and trapped in a sealed Abbey with no egress. A pair of the arabesque dancers thought to venture into through the broken glass and into one of the two corridors that ran parallel to the hall, but they were met by Elizabeth's followers.

Elizabeth remained alone in the black room, looking at the late Prince Propsero Malatesta. He had sought to create a world sealed off from the Red Death, or the great mortality, or the Black Death, as it was variously referred to. He had sacrificed his wife and her ladies in waiting in an effort to cheat the Black Death. No matter. Death came. Prospero's once so beautiful body was a gelatinous mass of soars and blood bursts.

"You don't look so attractive now."

***

A few of the revelers became fleshers as soon as or momentarily after they were bitten, and then they turned on their former partners, much to the dismay (and demise) of those partners.

Standing on the edge of the black room, Elizabeth noted the discrepancy. Why did some turn into fleshers right away while others did not? However, that was for later. The fleshers were feeding, and practically speaking, beyond her control. The fleshers were ravenous feeders and very difficult for Elizabeth, despite her powers, to control once there was blood on the floor. Even if a body was before them, they would go for the next breathing soul unless they were eating the brains or the entrails. The brains were the most delicious of delicacies and the prospect of a freshly killed one was maddening.

Elizabeth looked at the mask in her hand, then fitted it back onto her face. She walked slowly into the white room. The pure white of the carpet and the tapestry made a stark contrast with blood splattered across the carpet from fatty entrails that were being pulled out of the still living and feasted upon. Elizabeth walked through the rooms at a deliberate pace, each creature parting before her. In the center of the white room was Giancarlo, Elizabeth's old guard, sword drawn. His other men-at-arms lay dead around him, save for one who had turned and was ready to devour his former guard leader. Giancarlo was surrounded by other fleshers. Elizabeth walked towards him. The fleshers stood back.

Giancarlo had fought battles, but he now experienced fear as he never had. At Elizabeth's approach, he dropped his sword and fell to his knees, bowing his head, and clasped his hands in front of him.

"Milady." His voice was full of emotion.

Elizabeth stood above him and cocked her head. All around them as she spoke, the air filled with screams of agony and the sound of growls afeast.

"Yes, Giancarlo?" she asked.

"I betrayed you, choosing duty over my heart, and against your pleas. Ever since that night... I haven't stopped thinking of it."

Elizabeth stood before him, and asked, "Why?"

Giancarlo took a deep breath. "I-only-followed-the-orders. It was right... I told myself... but I didn't believe it."

"Whose orders?" Elizabeth asked. Still, she felt a twinge of pity.

Giancarlo remained frozen on the floor. "If you command it, I would fall on my sword. I deserve that."

"And put more blood on these beautiful carpets?" Elizabeth said.

"No need. Prince Prospero, my late husband, was persuasive. I understand. And you always treated me with dignity, even toward the end. Giancarlo, I could use someone like you to serve me. Would you be willing to do that?"

Giancarlo nodded.

She touched his shoulder and said, "Then, rise."

Trembling, yet looking her in the eye, Giancarlo stood.

Elizabeth said, "I do understand, Giancarlo, I do." She leaned into him and whispered, "But as I said long ago, *you made a choice."* She bit deep into his jugular, and her pupils burned orange.

***

Giancarlo thrashed on the floor for several minutes. Even with the flesher's insatiable blood lust, it was understood, in some manner, that none could attack this one. Elizabeth watched on with amusement and interest. The thrashing stopped. Giancarlo's eyes turned glassy, and he rolled onto all fours, issuing an indescribably inhuman sound.

Elizabeth flicked her hand and waived Giancarlo off to the black room, saying, "There's something in there you can eat."

Now a flesher, Giancarlo went scrambling on all fours toward the black room.

"Where you'll find Prospero," she said. A smile crossed Elizabeth's lips. "But there is still another to deal with."

***

All around Clarinda, the sounds of agonizing screams, mixed in with the tearing of flesh and the sound of teeth grinding through bones filled the air. Clarinda cowered on the carpeted dais of the orange apartment trying to hide behind the high chairs. From this room, the middle of the seven, she had not seen what had happened in the others, but she did not have to. She knew. She had always believed that she would not fear death when it came, that it would be a welcome release from the oppressiveness of life. But she had grown somewhat comfortable as the lady of the Abbey. Now that death was approaching, death in this most painful a form, she felt beyond fear. She recalled the warning she had been given–she could not hide from death, but she might *run* from it.

It was too late now. She raised her eyes upward. Her mind drifted, focusing on the single tripod suspended on the ceiling above her, just behind the orange stained glass.

Sounds grew dim. Mercifully, her mind was passing elsewhere.

Several hungry faces and arms came into view. It didn't matter. It would end soon. Already she felt numb and watched the scene from above, her soul ascending. What was happening below was not happening to her, it was only to the shell of what had been her body.

Suddenly, the room grew silent with only a guttural growl emanating from the back. Her mind was thrown mercilessly back into her body.

Dozens of hungry eyes were upon her, situated above mouths that dripped with blood and viscera. The horror was overwhelming. But then she became aware the harsh cry was coming closer to her.

The creatures divided to open a path between Princess Clarinda and the unholy mummer who had now reclothed itself with its grave cerements, and the mask of a corpse. Before when the figure had crossed the orange room, the mask had seemed blank and expressionless, but now it seemed to grin at her.

The mummer advanced.

Clarinda soiled her garments.

The figure removed its mask.

Clarinda gave a shriek and threw her arms to her face.

***

"You're dead!" Clarinda uttered.

Elizabeth bent over, took Clarinda's hands, and gently raised her to her feet.

Elizabeth spoke to her in a soft voice. "This seems so familiar, Clarinda, much like the last time we were together. You remember it, don't you? You are right, Clarinda. I am dead. But do not be afraid. You are the

Princess of this Abbey. You've presided over it, and you certainly bested me. You've taken my place. I honor thy royal blood with a kiss." With that, she touched Clarinda's quivering face and kissed each cheek. Elizabeth stepped back from her.

"Now go away." Clarinda moved one foot backward. No one else moved. Clarinda retreated another step. And another. One of the death creatures began to bend in toward her.

"Back," Elizabeth commanded aloud.

The creature still reached for Clarinda. There was a grasping motion made by Elizabeth. The ghoul grabbed its own head with both hands, wrenched it around, and then collapsed to the floor. The other ghouls fell further back from Clarinda. Elizabeth gestured with her fingers for Clarinda to turn. She did so and started to run.

She was unimpeded by the creatures. After a short way, she made it to the purple room. There she had to step over a disemboweled naked torso of creature with a single breast still attached to it, painted in brown. The woman who had been in the middle of the Ring Around the Rosie dance. One of the fleshers was gnawing on the innards of this body, like a hunting dog on a carcass. One of the creature's eyes had been damaged, but the other eye looked hungrily at Clarinda.

*Recognition.*

"Nicola!" Clarinda cried and brought her hands to her mouth.

There was a sting in her left hand. Looking into her palm, Clarinda saw something bloodied.

It was a ball of skin.

She dropped it. As it fell from her hand, the skin and muscle from her left pinky slid off the bone. A scream rose in her, but was choked in her throat and came out as a gaggle of blood. Her mouth seemed filled with liquid. She tightened her jaw and felt her front teeth crack into each other.

Clarinda touched her face, and her fingers broke through the skin. A wad of flesh caught under her clenched knuckles. The other creatures watched her hungrily, save for Nicola, who sat on her buttocks and observed.

Clarinda collapsed to her knees. Blood and urine and other bodily fluids oozed from various body cavities, both natural and others where her skin was splitting. When she opened her mouth, a sanguine mixture fell out.

Elizabeth spoke quietly.

"Now, Clarinda, go join my husband in hell."

Clarinda's body fell face forward. She lay prostrate on the carpet, her head turned to the side.

No comforting numbness came. She was completely aware of every inch of her pain.

Clarinda felt her optic nerve dissolve. Her right eye saw her left eyeball fall out of its socket, bounce briefly onto the purple carpet and roll away like a bloody marble. She did not see Elizabeth give a nod of approval to one, and only one, of the creatures on the floor. Clarinda Corrato's last vision was this particular creature–and in that final moment she knew it was Nicola–grabbing her eye and devouring it.

***

*Does the story continue? Of course.*

*But we have journeyed far tonight.*

*This tale is very tolling on the soul. Are you sure you wish me to go on?*

*So be it.*

# CHAPTER 21

*The Aftermath. What does Elizabeth still want?*

*Dawn. Five days later.*

***

ELIZABETH LED NICOLA UP a spiraling flight of stairs. "It's called *Scalone dei Morti*–the Staircase of the Dead," Elizabeth said. "An appropriate name, don't you think?"

Nicola made no sound but rested on her walking stick to ascend each step, first one foot, then another.

"That's good, that's good," Elizabeth cheered. "Slow progress is good."

This long, winding stairway (two hundred and forty-three steps to be exact, dear reader, but Elizabeth had lost the ability to count so high) curled through the northwestern part of the *Sacra di San Michele*.

Elizabeth wore a blue, silk kirtle, narrow at the waist, flowing at the ankles. The sleeves and the end of her dress were red and adorned with gold embroidery. Her recollection was not clear, but it was a dress she had loved when she was Elizabeth Malatesta. She had dressed Nicola in a red cotton dress with thin red straps across the shoulders that flowed. These clothes were for lounging. It was good to rest for a few days.

"All around us are niches and crypts," Elizabeth explained. "You can see the skeletons of the monks who lived here. You know, I didn't recall at first, but now I do. I walked this way before. Many times. We both did. In our past lives."

She had done this ascent thrice since reclaiming the monastery. Today with Nicola, she went at a much slower pace. Nicola sometimes tottered on a step, but Elizabeth would support her.

"You must keep moving," Elizabeth said, though Nicola could not understand. "When we slow down our bodies decay faster. We don't want that to happen just yet."

Their group's number had grown to nearly four hundred, including Giancarlo. While Elizabeth could not count so high, she knew it was growing into a force, and this gave her satisfaction. Almost as much as sending her husband to the next life. And her final resolution with Clarinda was the best of all.

"But now what?" Elizabeth said, adjusting a ribbon she had put in Nicola's hair.

The stairway ended in a great sculpted room, the Portal Zodiaco. A beautiful parapet led to another staircase, which they walked up. As they did, Elizabeth said "The sun will be strong this morning, and we are not covered, so we shan't stay long. But we have a little time."

Elizabeth helped Nicola navigate the last serpentine stairway and walk through the doorway. They walked out onto the highest parapet in the abbey, and found themselves in a thick mist.

"This is the most beautiful view of the Susa Valley, Nicola. On a clear day, you can see the French Alps. But this mist is preventing us from any of those views."

The temperature had changed rapidly overnight from a cool mid-spring night to a warmer dawn, which often caused a great fog to rise up and engulf the abbey on late spring mornings.

"Interesting," Elizabeth said, walking through the fog while Nicola shambled a few feet behind. "When we started it looked clear up here." They stopped several feet from the battlement walls, with its high merlons and deep cut crenelles.

"Let's not get too close, Nicola, we don't want to tumble over the edge," Elizabeth warned, breathing in the cool air. "I remember when we were tossed into that storm. I vowed to myself that if revenge were possible from beyond the grave, we would have it. Well, I think we found it. And you were a rock accompanying, me, silent then as now. I am most proud of you my dear lady-in-waiting." Elizabeth brushed Nicola's cheek.

Elizabeth ran her fingers through her own hair, then watched as a gust of wind from the *Val di Susa* blew red strands out from her palm.

"We're still dying, Nicola. A long, slow death." Elizabeth laughed. "Ah well, we've experienced it before!"

The fog seemed to grow thicker. There came a wind, billowing around the abbey's turrets.

Elizabeth thought she heard something in that breeze. In a loud voice, she called, "Death? Is that you?" She paused. Nothing. "Come out. Please, come out. We welcome you with open arms."

"Elizabeth," a voice sang. Female.

"One who died but is not dead," said a second voice. Familiar.

"One who does not wish to live but does not wish to die," said a third. Recognized.

Elizabeth walked through the fog toward the directions of the voices, pulling Nicola along by the arm.

Out of the mist appeared the form of three figures with hoods hiding their faces. They surrounded a shivering goat lying silent on the ground, its four feet tied together and leather straps tightly wound around its snout. One, the first, stood erect, and carried a Shepherd's crook. Another, the second, knelt by the goat, then took a knife and sliced open its belly. The third lay prone on the ground. As the viscera spilled from the quivering animal's abdomen, this one traced her finger in the blood that flowed onto the floor.

Elizabeth took them all in and casually observed, "Your cloaks drag on the ground."

All the figures pulled their hoods back to reveal the faces of young ladies, roughly Nicola's age. One shiny raven haired, one a brownish auburn, and one blonde.

Elizabeth took a step back, then paused. "Tell me my sisters–what do you want?"

"What do we want?" repeated the raven-haired one, standing with the crook.

"Why should we want?" asked the brown-haired one as she continued to cut the goat's carcass.

"What does Elizabeth want?" asked the blonde, using all her fingers on one hand to trace an elaborate design on the Abbey's stone floor.

Elizabeth laughed. "Young or old, you are mistresses of doubletalk But we are through. You wanted something from me, and I welcomed something from you. Whatever benefit I derived from coming here is my own. Whatever benefit you derived from it is your own. We are quite through."

"There is nothing Elizabeth wants" said the first, the black haired one, swaying back and forth while she held her stick.

"There is nothing Elizabeth wants?" said the second, questioning, still focused on the now-dead animal.

"Elizabeth does not know what she wants," observed the third, totally engrossed in her design.

The one with the Shepard's crook raised her eyes and met Elizabeth's, and then said "But we do."

"What do I want?" Elizabeth asked.

The blonde kept looking at her drawing and said, "That which you want we cannot tell."

The brunette pulled entrails from the goat and said, “That which you want we may or may not know.”

Elizabeth stormed forward and said, “Stop your games."

The raven-haired one suddenly appeared beside Elizabeth and wrapped the crook around Elizabeth’s. She said, “Though we cannot tell, and we may or may not know, we can *show*.”

Nicola’s arm slipped out of Elizabeth’s hand. Elizabeth turned and lost Nicola in the fog. Elizabeth stepped to go after her but was held by the shepherd’s hook which was still wrapped around her elbow. Elizabeth whirled to face the sister with burning orange eyes.

The black-haired sister met her gaze only inches from Elizabeth’s face, and said, “Nicola is not harmed.”

“She will not be harmed anywhere in this abbey,” said the brownish-auburn- haired one.

“You speak in riddles,” Elizabeth snarled.

“We do, we do.”

It was the blonde, and Elizabeth detected something unusual in her voice, especially when she continued by saying, “But for this moment, we speak frankly.”

Elizabeth looked to the blonde, then the brown one, and then back to the black-haired one who slid the shepherd’s crook off of Elizabeth’s elbow.

"You are free to go if you wish," said the black-haired one. "Or you can see what you want."

Elizabeth paused, but the black-haired one reached for Elizabeth's hand. Elizabeth allowed herself to be moved behind the blonde sister who still drew with her finger in the goat's blood, which was now spread on the floor. As Elizabeth looked down, the blood began to swirl. Colors other than red appeared and began to bleed together. Shapes formed.

In moments she was looking at the smoldering remains of a building.

"A church or a chapel," she observed.

"Look closer," said the blonde, sliding away and gesturing to the picture. Elizabeth got down on one knee and gazed deeper.

"Night has fallen," Elizabeth said, transfixed at the image. "The church is smoking. It was burned."

Behind her, a voice saying, "Look still deeper."

The air was filled with the smell of burnt timber. Her head felt heavy. She reached up and felt she was wearing some sort of helmet. Glancing down, she saw her body wore a triple level leather tunic covered in metal rings.

"Chain mail," she said.

She was seated on a large gray horse also draped in battle leather. Around her there were voices, muffled but growing clearer. The burned church was in front of her.

She was in the picture.

# CHAPTER 22

*October 9, 732 A.D.*

*Just before Midnight. Eastern Aquitaine, somewhere between the cities of Tours and Poitiers.*

***

CHARLES MARTEL PEERED THROUGH his helmet from atop his gray courser at the still smoking ruins of *Saint Hilaire de Grande*. The semicircular wall of the apse, which he knew housed many chapels, had been knocked down. No doubt, the Saracens had seen that was not defended and broke though there. Nothing was left of the roof save for a few burning timbers. The main walls still stood. Duke Eudes, similarly armored to Martel, was beside him on his black palfrey. Elizabeth could see all this through Martel's eyes. The familiar smell of smoke and burnt flesh reached her too,

"The Saracens are efficient," Martel said. "They've found and destroyed *Saint Hilaire de Grande* very quickly. Yet we cannot find them."

His words rang in Elizabeth's ears, yet she did not move her mouth. She could not.

"We cannot find them, but you commit our forces to the plains of *Moussais-la-Battaille*," the Duke responded nervously.

"Don't worry, my Duke," Martel said. "The governor of Cordoba will be there tomorrow."

"You must not do this," warned Duke Eudes. "What you seek here. It is blasphemy."

Martel smiled. "Yes, my Duke, it is. That is why we have come under cover of night with such a small force." He gestured back to eight other fighting men who sat atop their horses a respectful distance behind them. These were Martel's regulars, soldiers with cone-shaped spangenhelm helmets, scale armor, and reinforced gauntlets. Their shields were made from the highest quality oak, and he had armed them with longswords, lances, strong bows and quivers full of the best arrows. A small yet formidable band.

"We should not do this," Eudes repeated.

"No?" Martel glanced sideways at him. "My dear duke, your voice trembles."

"W-w-we must fall back," Eudes stammered. "We cannot–fight Al-Rahman's forces here."

"We cannot?" Martel asked with sarcasm.

Whatever the rumors said of Abd Al-Rahman being a vampire, he had assembled an undefeatable army thrashing armies through northern Africa and throughout Al Andalus, the Iberian Peninsula. Al-Rahman's cavalry annihilated three-fourths of Duke Eudes's–the best in the Carolingian Empire–at the Battle of the River Garonne. No doubt the experience had left the Duke a cringing shadow.

"We are mere men!" Eudes cried. "There is no shame in surrender. Mere men cannot defeat an army of vampires!"

Martel shook his head slightly. "No, mere men cannot." Then he reached for the reins on Eudes's palfrey and violently pulled the duke's face closer to his. Eudes's eyes bulged.

"I humbled you on the battlefield," Martel snarled. Then you tried to align with Al-Rahman and he overwhelmed you. You *lost Aquitaine* to the Berbers. Then you and Pope Gregory came to me, begging for an army to stop Al-Rahman." He shook the Duke. "Now my army and I are here. You think we should submit to them? What do you think would happen if we did? Do you think they would show you mercy?" He let the question hang for a minute. "Stop your sniveling. We don't turn back."

Martel released the reins. "Wait for me here." He dug in his heels and rode towards the burnt remains of the church.

***

As there was a full moon, along with flames, there was enough light to allow sufficient navigation. Martel rode around the remains of the church's exterior. The wooden roof had totally collapsed and more of the stone wall on the northern side had holes in them. What still stood was scorched. As he approached what must be the entrance, he came upon several bodies on the ground being cleaned by a few peasant women. Though it was midnight, the flames cast enough light to reveal their throats had been slashed.

Martel slowed his horse as he passed a woman stooping over the body of another woman. Though the field was filled with the disgusting odor of death, it was strangely quiet.

"I do not hear the groans of death." He made a sign of the cross.

The kneeling woman didn't look at him. "Because there must be living souls to make such sounds."

*She wears a wimple and a cross,* Martel thought. *A nun, perhaps?*

"The Abbey of St. Martins was destroyed. There was a nunnery there as well. Those who fled from St. Martins came here."

"I see what good it did them," Martel observed. "And who are you?

Still administering to the body, the woman answered, "A nun."

Martel turned. One of the other women stood behind him, silhouetted against fire still burning in the church.

"Survivors, there are none," this woman said.

"What will you do since this is done?" It was a third woman, also silhouetted against the flames.

Martel glanced around. All three now stood. He could see only their dark outlines.

They spoke in unison, "Will you save anyone?"

*My dear sisters, I didn't recognize you,* Elizabeth thought.

Martel said nothing but rode to the church entrance where he dismounted. He paused at the remains of two towers.

*The remaining walls seem higher in here than from the outside.*

He undid the strap under his chin, removed his domed spangenhelm helmet, and put it on the ground along with his shield and his chainmail byrnie. Martel crossed the narthex and walked into what had once been the central aisle of the church called *Saint Hilaire de Grande* .

His footsteps seemed to echo on the stone floor as if the church still stood intact. He looked back and forth as he walked until he reached the center transept and looked around.

To his right was a woman on her hands and knees scrubbing the ash-and-soot-covered stone floor with sponges next to a wooden bucket by her side. She wore a stained linen tunic, a coif, and her arms were covered with black soot.

*A Basque, no doubt,* he thought as he approached. *Why does she wash the floors so?* "You," he called. "Peasant woman. Why are you here?

The woman kept sponging the floor. "You. An uneducated bastard. Why are you here?"

Martel felt a chill. He almost spoke but caught himself recalling the seer's advice not to speak her name. Rather, he dropped to one knee and bowed his head. "You know why I am here."

"There is no need to kneel," replied the woman, who continued sponging in wide circling motions without looking at him. "I wish to hear it from you. So, I ask again, why are you here?"

Martel rose and cleared his throat, gathering his thoughts. *It is her.* "The Umayyads are fierce fighters," he began. "They have crushed all the armies of North Africa and Iberia and Al-Andalus. Now, Abd Al-Rahman, the Governor of Cordoba, has brought his army. It is the largest our land has ever seen. More than I have. They crossed over the Pyrenees and into Aquitaine. They smashed the army of Duke Eudes who then came crawling to me for help. And Abd Al-Rahman's army is somewhere outside of Mousssais-la-Bataille at the juncture of the Clain and Vienne Rivers, waiting to meet mine."

"And your army, they are positioned between those two rivers," the woman noted. "You are certain they will find you?"

Martel laughed. "We have searched for three days. They move like phantoms. So, I picked a spot of my own choosing and waited. Their scouts are excellent. They will find us."

"Your back is cut off from retreat by the two rivers," the woman said. "A tactical error on your part?"

Martel laughed again. "You understand battle tactics, my lady. I call it a calculated risk."

"And you question the quality of your Frankish army?"

"My regulars? No. They can match the Umayyads. But half of my army are stragglers, cobbled together from the dregs of the Carolingian Empire, fragmented as it is." Martel shrugged. "They are brawlers. The Saracens outnumber us, but I have found where to fight them. Against men, we would have a chance."

He paused.

The woman waited some time for Martel to complete his thought. "But what else?"

"The invaders have made a pact. Al-Rahman and his cavalry are vampires who feast on blood. Stronger and faster than my best men. The vampires only form part of his army, maybe four thousand strong, but they are enough."

"Will not the sun weaken them?" the woman asked.

"They fight in the sun," Martel said. "The sun may diminish their powers, but they still battle well."

"And you have no strategy against them?

"Oh, we have a few tricks for the Saracens." Martel smiled, then shook his head, adding, "But not enough."

"So, you come seeking my aid to defeat them? "Yes."

The woman continued to sponge the floor. Martel noticed her entire body was caked with soot and ashes

"You are uneducated but not without wisdom," she began. "Your assessment of the Saracen army is correct. When Abd Al-Rahman defeats and kills you tomorrow–which he will–there will be nothing to stop him. His armies will conquer not only Aquitaine but Neustria, then Burgundy, Austrasia, Lombardy, Swabia–even Frisia. There will be nothing to stop his triumph."

The woman stopped scrubbing, then added, "And I do not wish that to happen."

Martel contemplated this statement. "Then why do you not strike Al-Rahman down?"

The woman went back to her work. "There are rules, limitations, from a greater power even I must follow. I cannot create history." She paused. "But I can *influence* it."

Martel listened for more, but after some time he said, "I am, as you say, an uneducated bastard. You know I seek your help. Can you provide it–and if so, will you?"

The woman dropped her sponge and stood. The soot slid from her body and clothing. Her clothes shimmered and transfigured into a flowing, immaculate purple tunic with long sleeves and gold trim. She put her hands to her lips for silence, then reached into one sleeve and produced a small glassine bottle which she lay on the spot of the stone where she had been washing. Then she began to walk upward, ascending a non-existent stairwell. When she was several times his height in the air, she stopped.

"On the battlefield tomorrow, you must use all your skills to defeat the Saracens. And during battle when you are struck with a mortal wound, at the point of death, you must drink this."

Martel started to reach for the bottle, then pulled his hand back. "I come to you, and you offer me this vial of liquid? A bottle smaller than my hand?" He had castrated men for insults before, both foes and insubordinate men. Martel kicked and smashed several pieces of burnt rubble with his gloved hands.

"You display audacity before me?" the woman asked calmly.

Martel scowled but ceased.

"I was waiting for your famed temper to appear," the woman continued. "You have asked for my help. This is what I offer. The choice to take it or not is yours."

Martel stared at the container.

"My time is short," she said. "While your request is most interesting to me, it is not the only one, and I have other places to visit. Do you take my offer of assistance or not?"

Martel reached for the ampule but stopped short of touching it. "Do you visit the Saracens tonight?" he asked.

"No."

Martel grabbed the flask. It felt like–a small vial of liquid.

"You do not ask the price," she commented.

Martel took a quiet breath. "It will be exorbitant. I knew that when I decided to seek you out." He looked up at her. "I must pay it."

"Even if the cost is your life?"

Martel's eyes opened wide. "Yes. If we lose tomorrow, we will be dead. Any who runs will be hunted down like the nuns and monks of Saint Martin's who lay outside. The Frankish life will die. If we fight, this will be remembered as the greatest battle in the history of the Francs. If we can defeat the enemy, I will be known as the savior of all Gaul.

The chance for that glory–however slim– is worth dying for."

The woman smiled, and even Martel, as battle-hardened as any man in Aquitaine, felt a chill. "Then we have an agreement." Her image grew blurred. An aura was forming around her. "If you win, you will see me again tomorrow." As the woman dematerialized, he heard the words, "Remember, only drink the liquid at the point of death."

***

*October 10, 732 A.D.*

*Sunrise. Moussais-la-Battaille, a large field roughly wedged between the Clain and Vienne Rivers.*

"Steady men!" Martel cried, riding along the front of his army, trailed by Duke Eudes and the same detachment that had accompanied him to Saint Hilaire. The army was assembled on a short rise in front of a forest. Four thousand infantrymen knelt just atop the ridge, another four thousand men standing behind them. Behind those massed a larger group, a rabble, about fifteen to eighteen thousand total. In front of them spread a wide plain.

If his plan went smoothly, the rivers to his far right and left would funnel the Saracens up the rise toward his lines and cut off their retreat. A rider going at full pace would ascend the hill swiftly, but the height should slow his horse's stride. True, a line formation had never withstood a mounted attack, but he had no cavalry of his own, just a small number of horse soldiers, the remnants of Eudes' calvary. This was the best position Martel could choose.

Meanwhile, he had posted contingents of archers on the flanks of the tree line, no more than four hundred strong. These good Franks could send about three, perhaps four volleys before their foe reached the tree line, but they had flat bows. The Saracens' best archers could fire six volleys with their composite bows. Surely their scouts must know all this by now.

Martel rode his horse to the middle of his vanguard and stopped about forty paces in front so he could be seen up and down the line. Every single man was still.

*He holds absolute command over his army,* Elizabeth observed. *They fight with him knowing the overwhelming odds.*

The men in the first line kneeled on the thick grass.

Martel called, "Front row. Show your swords."

They held their Carolingian swords high, both short and long. Straight blades of good stern iron, narrow and tapered.

"Second row. Raise your weapons!"

The men in the second line lifted their long-handled spears, their halberds, and long-poled weapons topped with an axe blade and a spike on the other. Most of these men wore spangenhelm helmets, chainmail byrnies, and carried round wooden shields covered in leather.

"Remember your training," he called again. "Listen to my commands." His voice carried far over the silent formation.

Elizabeth kept her eyes on him. *You command your army with authority, Charles Martel. But is that enough to defeat a vampire army?*

***

Martel had only seen the ocean once in his life, when he was eleven years old. He remembered being fascinated by the motion of waves, curling up, growing and spreading in length until they turned and crashed onto the shore. He thought of this as he and Duke Eudes surveyed the Umayyad army advance across *Moussais-la-Battaille*.

The heavy scimitars of the Saracens glinted in the early morning sun. They formed a row longer than the tree line on the other side of *Moussais-la-Battaille* where Martel's army waited. The Umayyads rode slowly atop beautiful Arabian stallions, a sea of grays and whites, with the morning sun reflecting off the Saracen's helmets and armor. Some carried long staffs hanging plain white field flags, bearing the crescent of the Umayyad Caliphate.

Martel adjusted the mail coif which he now wore with the battle imminent. "They seem in no hurry, do they, my Duke?"

Duke Eudes did not respond.

"Of course, they have no need to," Martel continued, answering his own question. "Their horses are Andalusians. Beautiful animals, don't you think? And in the open field, faster than our coursers. But I like our coursers and our rounceys in a fight."

Duke Eudes remained silent.

"I wonder, Duke, are we closer to Tours, to Poitiers? Is this the Battle of Tours, or the Battle of Poitiers?"

The Duke stammered "I-I- not..."

Martel raised a gauntlet-covered hand. "I think Tours is closer, but–what does it matter?" He circled his horse to the side.

Elizabeth eyed the fear on Eudes's face, awaiting Martel's next words as if waiting for an executioner's blade to fall. Why did Martel even have him here?

"You're a good soldier. I have faith in you, my Duke. Go to the rear and execute our plan."

Eudes turned his palfrey and went back through the Frankish lines.

Martel fixed his eyes back on Al-Rahman at the front of the Umayyad line. The Governor leaned forward on his mount, his shoulders square and massive. Tales of the man had been wild and fanciful. Men called him a force of destruction on the battlefield. His strength was apparently a match for a tiger. He was said to have laughing eyes which were glued on Martel at the moment. And his tactical cunning came from an intimate understanding of fear and discomfort.

Al-Rahman placed his vampires in the front of the assault.

Even from a great distance, Martel could see a hungry look in the eyes of the Arabian cavalry in the first line. He felt a knot of fear in his stomach but quickly banished it. He raised his gauntlet and made a beckoning motion for the Governor of Cordoba.

Al-Rahman raised his sword in a salute. Then he sliced the air.

The Saracen cavalry increased the pace of their advance.

Martel spun his horse to the men, raised his sword, and slashed. "EYES DOWN."

His soldiers bowed their heads.

***

Even in the bright sun, Al-Rahman's keen eyesight saw the helmets of the men in Martel's first two lines bend.

*Interesting,* Al-Rahman thought. The Moors's approach was designed to strike fear into the opposing forces. Martel had his men ignore the sight of the oncoming cavalry.

*You can have your army avert our eyes. But you cannot close your ears.*

Al-Rahman raised his silver scimitar again and aimed forward. This time, the Umayyad cavalry charged at full speed.

***

Martel felt the ground beneath his horse shake. Thirty thousand hoof beats pounding the field sounded like thunder. Martel pointed his sword to the far right and left. Arrows fell on the advancing Saracens. None could strike many fatal blows, but they disrupted the rider or the horse enough. Some riders fell, and those behind them crashed.

Still, the wave kept coming. The Andalusian horses were quick and agile, their riders skilled. As the arrows from the second volley were still in the air, the Saracen cavalry spread out, the front riders charging faster while others slowed to create space between them. The extra spaces allowed some to avoid an arrow or a fallen rider in front of them. The second volley did strike home on some, but fewer than the first. The vampire cavalry continued their ride.

Behind them, the foot soldiers followed—mere mortals, but still great fighters. A third volley went, but even before it landed, Martel turned his horse and rode back to the second line where he dismounted and again raised his sword.

Martel signaled for the fourth volley of arrows to be held.

The Saracen cavalry approached the Frankish army.

"HOLD YOUR POSITION!" Martel yelled.

The Umayyad cavalry had reached the rise. The riders pushed their horses up the small incline.

"SWITCH!" Martel shouted as loud as he had ever uttered a word.

The kneeling soldiers dropped their swords and reached into the tall grass for wooden lances they had laid there. The cavalry drove forward up the small hill and into the tree line. Each of the kneeling men thrust the base of the lance into the small hole they had dug, clutched their lance with both hands, and raised the wooden tip of the lance skyward.

As the vampire cavalry reached the rise, they ran into a row of wooden lance tips, all angled up. With no time to stop, many of them rode into the lances. The wooden tips pierced their leather armor, impaling the vampire riders through the heart.

***

*October 10, 732 A.D.*

*Midday. In the middle of Moussais-la-Battaille.*

The battle had waged for hours. Martel's maneuver had sizably reduced the Saracen vampires. More than half of the Umayyad front riders had been skewered and killed or mortally wounded the moment they reached the front line. The speed of the Andalusian horses worked against the cavalry, for the second line had moved in and collided with many of the riders of the first wave, and there was no room atop the rise to maneuver. Many of the riders in the front fell onto the second wave. Many who tried to turn fell into the rider beside them.

*Successful,* Elizabeth thought. *But you have not won the battle, only cut down a sizeable portion of the Saracen cavalry.*

Foot soldiers from both sides moved onto the flat field, along with the remaining cavalry, engaging in the brutal medieval combat Charles had so much experience with. Dead and dying bodies along with severed limbs, torsos, and heads were so numerous it was hard to move on the field without falling. The Franks were fighting furiously, but Al-Rahman had rallied his men and organized a counter-offensive with his surviving cavalry and the wave of foot soldiers on the plain.

Man for man, the Saracen, and the Frankish warriors were equal, but the vampires, though roughly a thousand in number, tipped the scales. In the closeness of battle, one could kill a vampire by beheading it or ripping its heart out. An especially strong Frankish warrior might give the vampire a battle and a group of men could kill one. But as the battle continued, bodies dropped, and more space appeared between the combatants leading to more single encounters. In these one-on-ones, each vampire won more than they lost.

Standing on the plain, Martel clutched his sword. His horse had been killed after the first hour. His helmet and mail coif were long gone. Blood ran down his face from a gash he had been given by the edge of a Saracen shield. Around him were many dead and dying from both sides, and the stench of death was everywhere.

"Martel!"

Martel turned.

Al-Rahman looked at him from atop his mount, holding a scimitar. Several of his vampire aides, including Tariq Musa and the scout Zaid Jafar, were on horses behind him. Al-Rahman moved his stallion forward and motioned his vampires to stay back.

Martel glanced around for a shield or a battle axe but saw none. He clenched the hilt of his sword with both hands.

"You are a fine commander," Al-Rahman called out.

Martel spoke between heavy breaths, "You speak—Aquitaine—very well, Governor."

Al-Rahman raised his curved sword.

"Remember, Charles, you must strike me in the heart or the head. That is the only way you will ever stop me."

Martel tightened the grip on his sword.

Al-Rahman charged.

Martel's swing gashed Al-Rahman above his heart, across his chest, hopefully to his abdomen. He couldn't be sure, it was all too fast. Al-Rahman rode by and stopped his horse, looked at his wound, and coughed. He slid to the ground. For a moment, Martel thought he had killed him.

But then, Al-Rahman stood, blood pumping from his slit chest.

"A serious blow," the Governor breathed heavily, leaning on his horse. "But not enough."

Martel's sword felt heavy in his hand. It was covered in blood—two different hues. And fresh drops were falling on it. Martel dropped it and felt his throat. Blood was leaking from his neck.

"Your bloodline," Al-Rahman said.

His own attack had come so precisely, so quickly, Martel never saw it. He collapsed onto his hands and knees. His vision grew dim. Around him he heard nothing. He fell onto his side and felt cold. Very cold. Then his eyes closed.

*The liquid.*

With his body stiffening and his heartbeat racing, Martel reached under what little was left of his mail and clasped the small wine sack he had wrapped the bottle in. Unable to see, he removed the cotton batting he had stuffed in the bottle and brought it to his lips.

He drank.

His heart beat two more times. And then it ceased.

*This is it then?* Elizabeth wondered.

Suddenly, Martel could see. Within. Within his body. He could see his heart. From his years on the battlefield, he had seen many of the body's inner parts and recognized what a heart looked like. He could see his heart stop beating.

*No.*

His heart began to beat again.

He felt the bloodlines in his neck and saw the torn flesh around them. He willed the tubes to close. The muscle, scapular, and trapezoid (not that he knew the names, but he recognized them from the battlefield) that had been cut reassembled themselves. Slowly at first, then quicker. He made the muscles reform. He willed the tissue to reconnect. He felt blood gushing through his body, and anywhere there was a wound, the blood flowed in, and he *willed* the wounds close. The skin healed, and there was no mark left.

He commanded his body. Fresh strength filled him.

Martel sprang to his feet and looked at Al-Rahman. From the governor's open chest wound, he could smell his foe's blood dripping out. Somehow his nose pushed past the smells of battle and latched onto the Governor's blood. It seemed vampire blood had a tinge of green in it, a hue he had not noticed before. And more, he sensed into Al-Rahman's mind. There was... fear at seeing that which he never had before.

*Elizabeth could smell the blood too and knew it was vampire. But this ability to see into the body and heal it so rapidly, she had never experienced that.*

"How?" Al-Rahman uttered.

Martel ran toward him with no weapon in hand.

Al-Rahman hesitated but quickly climbed back on his horse and charged. He swung his scimitar in a low, sweeping motion, but Martel dove under the blade and grabbed the Saracen's arm from behind. Al-Rahman was pulled off his horse and lost his weapon, but he quickly scrambled to his feet. He was partly hunched over, holding his hand over his still-bleeding chest wound. Martel could see the blood being pumped by the heart and pushed through the vampire's wounds.

And he wanted it.

Al-Rahman bared his fangs the way a cornered dog might face a bear. Martel eyed him with a stronger hunger than a vampire. But Al-Rahman had sliced open Martel's throat moments ago. Most of his body armor had fallen, exposing an unblemished torso after three hours of fighting. Al-Rahman reached down and picked up a short sword. He gripped it with both hands.

"Your magic is powerful," he called.

"Prepare yourself," Martel called back. There was a large battle axe among the dead which he picked up with one hand.

From their horses Al-Rahman's second, Tariq Musa, and his officers saw the Frankish leader rush their Governor. They saw Martel nimbly running over the bodies showing no fatigue. Al-Rahman appeared ready to slice across Martel's body, but at the last moment, he raised his sword overhead and sliced down, trying to split Martel in two. Martel jumped to the side and swung his axe.

Al-Rahman's head flew off the neck and bounced on the ground before stopping against a dead horse.

The Saracen leader's decapitated body stood for a moment before toppling to the ground.

While the seconds stared at their leader's body, Martel ran across the field and pounced onto Zaid Jafar, the chief vampire scout, knocking him off his mount. They wrestled on the ground until Martel bit deep into his throat. Jafar made a gasping sound, and his body rattled. Martel felt something inside himself transfer to the scout. Then he let Jafar go. Somehow the scout managed to climb to his feet

Tariq Musa had regained control of his frightened horse. He pointed his scimitar with his left hand towards Martel and said "Destroy—"

Before he could finish, the bitten scout grabbed Musa's right leg and gnawed into the femur. The second screamed as blood spurted. His sword couldn't reach Jafar so he hit him with his gloved hand, but the scout would not release his jaws from Musa's leg. The others watched as the second's horse rose on its hind legs and threw his rider to the ground. After wrestling with each other, the scout stopped and looked at the other riders. Musa also got up. Their eyes were covered with a dull glaze.

One of the surviving scouts cried out in Arabic, "Kill them both." He drove his horse towards the two, expecting others to follow, but he glanced back and saw no one came with him. His horse tripped over another of the many bodies on the field and both horse and rider fell to the ground. The horse struggled to get up but its right front leg was broken. The rider lay pinned, trying to wriggle out, but the animal's weight was too much.

Then Musa and the scout were on him while Martel watched serenely.

A Saracen warrior, carrying only a spear, burst out of a melee and ran toward him. Martel smiled. He could see himself from the soldier's perspective. He could see the man's hands tightly clenched around the spear's shaft, its head angled right at the Frankish commander.

*Stop*, Martel whispered into the soldier's mind, and the soldier immediately did so.

Martel quietly walked over and bit into the Saracen's right bicep.

He liked its taste.

# CHAPTER 23

*October 10, 732 A.D. The middle of Moussais-la-Battaille. Approaching dusk.*

***

Martel sat on the battlefield, his body saturated in the blood of others, but underneath that, his own body was pristine, save for one gash on his forearm that he was in the process of healing.

*It is an unusually quiet battlefield*, he remarked to himself. There was not the usual cacophony of groans and cries of agony from dying men. No, those on the field who lay fallen were most definitely dead. Bodies of men and horses were everywhere. Of course, the air reeked with the smells of the lifeless, which drew both looters and the women who came to cleanse the bodies.

Martel felt... invigorated.

A woman's voice came to him.

"You're thinking this is like the scene you saw outside the chapel where we met last night."

"Yes," Martel said, then added, "and no. The dead here are my soldiers mixed with those of my enemy."

Looking up, he saw the woman from last night hovering off the ground. She wore a pristine white tunic and a gold headdress adorned with glowing jewels.

"As a young bastard, I saw drawings by monk who tried to teach me of the supposed Greek gods," he said. "You remind me of one such picture."

"But I am not," The woman sounded amused. Then she added, "The Umayyads have withdrawn."

Martel chuckled. "I never studied the discipline of math, but that same monk once tried to teach me. I remember the idea that if one piece of wood splits into two pieces, and then the two pieces split into four, and so on, then even though you have the same amount of wood, the number of pieces grow quickly. I thought it interesting but meaningless information. Today, I see I was wrong."

"I watched you," the woman told him. "As a Saracen warrior was turned, that one turned on another, and so on. Some of the Saracens were eaten, but enough turned on the others. You were fortunate that most of the vampire army stayed near Al-Rahman. And you controlled them. Once they became flesh eaters. Which I foresaw. But you had Eudes take smaller cavalry of the Franks and swim the horses across the Clain River. I had not foreseen that."

Martel shook slightly at the words. "Surprised the Duke didn't drown himself." Then he shrugged. "But then again, palfreys are better swimmers than war horses."

The woman crossed her arms. "Having them swing around and cross farther up, a pincer movement around the battlefield to the Umayyad's camp. That was brilliant. And then Eudes' men – you had them release the Umayyad servants."

Martel smiled. "With the Saracens between us on one side and their newly freed servants on the other, with Eudes calvary support in the rear – I don't think Al-Rahman saw that coming."

"You slaughtered nearly all the vampires and freed their servants, but you allowed much of the other Saracens to escape. Why?"

Martel breathed deeply before responding. "I must correct you slightly. When the Saracens turned into – whatever was in that bottle – the vampires slaughtered each other. Once they were eliminated, the others wanted no more of this battle. Fear of the undead is quite strong. Fear of the looting their treasure was, perhaps, greater. They've fallen back with their spoils and are heading to their base in the Pyrenees."

"A tactical draw on the battlefield, but a strategic victory for you Franks." the woman observed.

Martel nodded. "There was no need to do more."

He rose to his feet, feeling relaxed. "So, I have lived to meet you again. You are here to claim your price. Do so."

The woman descended to the ground and walked around Martel.

"The price is complicated and beyond your complete understanding. But I shall explain to you as best you can understand. You have stopped the Saracen invasion of Neustria. That is your victory. It also works for my interests. So, your victory was part of my price. You may not understand, but victory itself is a price to pay, sometimes even more than defeat."

Martel listened carefully. "Every battle victory has a cost. Go on."

"Second, you know the taste of flesh. And you experienced how to repair your body. Yet you shall never be able to use this power again. Oh, it will remain in you. Dormant, so to say, but present. You shall sire children, and they shall sire children, and the power will be passed down, but it will not appear as you have held it now. Not for many generations. Oh, occasionally, a portion may be seen. You will have a grandson who you will not live to see, who shall have the greatest tactical mind on this earth, even greater than yours. But, he shall also be refined in a way you are not. He shall unite the Franks into an empire much greater than you can imagine, the largest of his day. You will know this but not live to see it. This knowledge is also a price."

The woman laughed. "But your grandson's empire shall last only for the duration of his life. As I said, the powers will appear on occasion, but they shall not manifest themselves all the time. And your grandson's children will not exhibit the same brilliance as their father. The powers will be in your bloodline but diluted with each generation. Your lineage shall sire many, both legitimate and bastards. And you now know this, and that knowledge is a price."

Martel nodded.

"And?"

"Someday – far from now, very far from now – there will be a chance for another to be even more powerful than you. An aberration, if you will. Your many crossed bloodlines will converge in her, purely by chance. She will be most interesting."

"She?" Martel asked.

The woman smiled as she nodded, and Martel saw a spark in her eyes.

"Yes, she. But to achieve the highest powers, she will need to find and conjoin with the blood of three others who will, like her, appear by chance as the next purest blood descendants. Another bastard like you, but a woman and her two children, who may be a young girl and a boy. This will lead to a new and exciting game which may be... eventful."

"Eventful?" Martel questioned. "May be? You do not know?" He paused in thought before adding, "You seem interested in happenings far in the future."

"I am not truly immortal, but my life is long," the woman replied. "I need to keep myself interested. And while I set things in motion, nothing is certain. I am not omnipotent. You cannot comprehend it all – though to be frank, I believe you understand more than I thought you would. Today, we have put things in motion which may come to pass."

The woman stopped in front of Martel.

"Time is transient. For instance, the one to be born so far into the future, the one with the hunger for flesh that you had – she might hear us, even now."

The woman looked directly into Martel's eyes. For a moment, he thought – *no, he sensed* – another presence within her, like a shadow passing over her face.

*She's looking at me,* Elizabeth realized. *She is the master of the three sisters.*

A swirl of dust swirled the woman's feet and then began to rise, encircling her, blotting her from his view. "You are an interesting man, Charles Martel. Live well."

Dust filled Elizabeth's vision. She felt her eyes sting. Then she found herself standing in the middle of the parapet atop Sacra di San Michele.

***

The three sisters were gone, but Nicola was beside her. The fog had dissipated. Elizabeth grasped Nicola's arm. "Nicola, where are they?"

Then the raven-haired one was beside her.

"The woman and the two children will travel in a caravan of Papal envoys from Rome to Avignon. The mother is named Emilia Barberini, the boy is called Bartolome, and the girl is Maddalena. The mother was born in a brothel, and she is now a consort. The boy is a bit simple. The girl is slightly older than her brother but most perceptive and keenly observant. Yet like the others, she has no idea of her ancestry. In two weeks, you may be able to find them by the Po River. Be warned, if they are killed, you will not be able to partake in their blood more than once unless you quickly preserve the body. We can show you how. But it is better if they are alive. And if you only partake once, your ability to heal yourself will be temporary, and after some time, you will return to be as you are."

Elizabeth stared at the sister for a long time. "You speak frankly, for once. Why do you tell me this?"

"That is our concern, not yours," said the black-haired one.

"And if I choose not to pursue these three?" Elizabeth asked.

"That is your choice, not ours," The sister smiled and backed away. Elizabeth felt Nicola a tug on her shoulder and glancing over, she saw Nicola holding her other arm. When Elizabeth looked back, the sister was gone.

As Elizabeth stared at the Susa Valley, her mind swirled with images of roads she had traveled, roads which led to the Po River.

"Janosz Ujvary!" Elizabeth called, bursting into a church in the abbey from the stairway of the dead. Janosz and some of the others had found three survivors from the other night hiding in a secret compartment behind a fresco of Michael the Archangel. These were quickly dispatched, but Janosz did not feed. Rather he let the others do so. He had eaten. His interest had been satisfied by finding others.

Now he just sat, waiting in the Navata Destra, the right aisle of this church, sitting straight, his hands resting on his knees, with his head slumped down slightly.

"Janosz," she said again, grabbing his shoulder. The hulking figure slowly got to his feet.

"We're not going to die again, after all!" Elizabeth said, her voice animated. "We need to find a family. A mother and two children. They are not far. And we will find them, Janosz. I promise we will."

Her face was alive, and the iris of her eyes burned orange. "And then, won't that be fun."

***

*And here, our story ends. My, we have spoken for some time. The night is well past compline, and prime is beginning to appear. I must bid you good night.*

*Ahh, you are most insistent and a rapt listener. Very well. We have time for a glimpse - and just a glimpse - into the next tale in this saga.*

# Epilogue

*A new adventure begins*

*Somewhere by a river in northwestern Italy, near the French border.*

*A young girl not quite on the cusp of womanhood, but approaching, is picking flowers by the water.*

***

I LIKE THE FIRETHORNS. The red flowers. Here on the riverbank. I have a handful which I will give to Mother.

"The prettiest ones are the highest," said a woman.

I had not seen her coming. She was hunched over, dressed in scarves and tattered clothes. A Romani wanderer.

"The higher ones have thorny branches around them," I said.

The woman shuffled toward me. Her skin had a strange color to it.

"Don't be afraid, my dear," she said. "I only want to see what you have picked."

*Should I run?* Mother said to be careful of strangers. But my caravan was near. I could yell if I needed to. I tilted my hand and showed the Romani woman my flowers.

"Very pretty," she said. "Like you."

I smiled but I was still not happy the woman was here. I noticed she seemed unable to straighten her body.

"Would you like these?" I asked. "They are for my mother, but I can pick more."

"No, give them to your mother," said the gypsy. "But that one—at the top of the shrub." She pointed up. There was a very large bloom at the peak. A shade of pink with bright red trim.

"I cannot reach it," she continued. "Would you pick it for me?"

I leaned into the bush and reached high. The branches brushed against my arms. I could almost reach it. I grasped the stem and twisted it. My arm scratched against the thorns in the thicket.

"Ouch," I said, pulling my arm down and handing the flower to the gypsy.

"Oh, thank you," she said, taking them from my hand. "But you are bleeding. I'm sorry. Let me see."

The woman reached for my arm and then licked the scratches. Several times. I would not have let her do it, but I did not know what she would do. After a moment, the cuts stopped bleeding, and there was no sting.

The woman smiled at me, and said, "Behold."

I look down and—the scratches were healing. Right in front of me. In moments, my cut was healed. I stared at my arm, then looked at the woman.

"How did you do that?" I asked.

"Gypsy magic, my dear," she said.

Her skin—it seems less pale. Healthier.

I looked at the firethorn flower and said, "I like it."

The gypsy smiled at me. "So do I." She handed me the flower. "Keep this for yourself. I want you to have it." She started to shuffle away. With her back turned, she asked, "Are your mother and brother nearby?"

"Yes, up and over the hill," I answered.

"Then you should go back to them," she said. "Goodbye."

"Goodbye," I said. I started to go back up the hill, and I heard her ask, "What is your name, child?"

"Maddalena," I called back.

I headed back to our wagons. But then I paused and turned. The woman was nowhere to be seen.

How did she know I had a brother?

***

*Thank you for listening to my tale. I enjoy telling my stories, and so seldom do I have a listener as avid as you.*

*Is there more? There is always more. One story leads into the next. The sun sets and it then rises. Like this night, this drama is through.*

*What? The young girl Maddalena? What became of her?*

*That is a much longer story for another time. Come again, and perhaps we shall speak of her.*

# AUTHOR'S NOTE

GIOVANNI BOCCACCIO WAS AN Italian writer of the 14th century and a keen observer of the human condition. He lived from approximately 1313 A.D. to 1375 A.D. His most famous work today is (almost certainly) "The Decameron," an anthology of one hundred stories broken into ten general concepts or themes, told by one of ten different narrators. These tales, though written around or shortly after what we reference today as "The Black Death," do not really involve the Black Death or what was often referred to as the "Great Pestilence". The frame story, however, which Boccacio used to set up his ten narrators, is set at the height of the sickness, in Florence, circa 1348 A.D. Boccaccio's frame story, which today we might call a prologue, shows us how contemporaries of the time saw this sickness.

His description of the appearance of boils on the body, their spread, and the additional appearance of the black or purple blotches is a first-hand account of the sickness's entrance into Florence. It is a more frightening piece of writing than any fictional work. Of the efforts of doctors, physicians, and others, both learned and those pretending to be so, none were able to come up with an effective understanding of what this illness was, and how to combat it.

One of the most prevalent medical beliefs of the time was that the human body was composed of four substances or humors—blood, phlegm, yellow bile, black bile. These terms were used a bit differently than what we might call them today, but the belief was that illness was caused by an imbalance of the four humors. Medical treatments would be based on adjusting these imbalances. However, they would not be very beneficial, other than rest. People had no concept of what a virus was.

According to Boccaccio, people learned on their own that proximity and contact with the infected could lead to the spread of the illness. Some attempted to avoid the disease by fleeing the cities, running away, or shutting themselves up in the city and sealing off the outside world. To do either, it would be helpful to have resources, financial and otherwise.

The ten tellers of tale in "The Decameron" are described as nobles who leave from Florence into the countryside to wait out the plague. This tactic *might* work, if one was able to isolate and not come into contact with a person infected. We cannot be certain today how long a person could be infected and not show signs of illness. People like Prospero would also see bringing in healthy-looking people as a way to make the place safe. Health was judged by appearance, which is why it was easy to convince Giancarlo to remove the clearly sick Elizabeth.

Of course, Prospero's interests laid towards hedonism and ego satisfaction more than general health and safety, but that's another matter.

Of course, a well-known theory is that much of the plage was carried by rodents, rats in particular, on whom fleas (and it is suggested ticks) containing the cause of the illness clung to. People in the 14$^{th}$ century lived in greater proximity to their animals than we do today, so one cannot discount what that might have to do with the spread of the disease. Today, we cannot be entirely certain of how or why the Black Death spread so quickly.

# ABOUT THE AUTHOR

William J. Connell is currently a practicing attorney in the great states of Rhode Island and Massachusetts. He has also worked as a public school teacher in the areas of Special Education and History in the same states. He enjoys writing on a wide variety of topics. Most of his non-fiction material is in the legal field, and his work has been published in many law journals, most frequently in The Rhode Island Bar Journal. His fiction tends to run to historical adventure, which reflects his love of teaching history, mixed with elements of sci-fi, classic literature, and horror thrown in for good measure!

Besides being a member of the Wild Ink Writing Family, for which he is most grateful, he has had fiction pieces published by The Ravens Quoth Press, Godless Publishers, Culture Cult Press, and Underland Press. He likes to spend time with his family and Lulu, the family's green-cheeked conure. His author/writer website continues to be a leading example of why you should not do one yourself unless and until you know what you are doing.

Printed in the USA
CPSIA information can be obtained
at www.ICGtesting.com
LVHW090038071224
798547LV00001B/42

*9781958531938*